THIS BOOK BELONGS TO

Aladdin took the lighted lamp from
the niche (page 112)

"Is it time?" asked the thief from within
the jar (page 42)

TALES FROM THE
ARABIAN NIGHTS

TALES FROM THE
ARABIAN NIGHTS

Illustrated by A. E. Jackson

Bounty
Books

First published in 1990 by Ward Lock Limited

This edition published 2005 by Bounty Books,
a division of Octopus Publishing Group Ltd,
2-4 Heron Quays, London E14 4JP

ISBN   0 7573 1095 1
ISBN 13   9780753710951

Printed and bound in Slovenia

CONTENTS

LIST OF ILLUSTRATIONS

THE STORYTELLER

nce, long, long ago, a Sultan, whose name was Shahriar, ruled over a kingdom as large as India. He had a wife to whom he was fondly attached and who, he thought, loved him fondly in return.

But one day he discovered that his Sultana cared for him so little that she even preferred the company of a black slave. His rage on this discovery was so great that he ordered her to be put to death, and declared that he would never again trust a woman.

Consequently, as he did not like to remain single, he married a new wife every day, and had her put to death the following morning.

Now the Grand Vizier, or Prime Minister, had two daughters, whose names were Sheherazade and Dinarzade. The elder, in addition to being very beautiful, was very clever and intelligent. She had an amazing memory, and never forgot anything she read or heard.

In fact, she possessed almost every virtue, could do

no wrong, and was the apple of her father's eye.

One day, when the Grand Vizier was looking extremely worried because so few suitable young ladies were left, his daughter, Sheherazade, came to him and said:

"My father, I have a special request."

"Ask, my child," he replied, "and if the request is reasonable, which, coming from you it is sure to be, you may consider it granted."

"Then, my dear father," said Sheherazade, "let *me* be the Sultan's next wife."

The Grand Vizier was at first struck dumb and breathless with horror. When he had recovered, he did his best to persuade his daughter to change her mind. But Sheherazade persisted and persuaded and coaxed the poor man until, much against his will, he agreed that she should have her way.

Even the Sultan himself was surprised when the Grand Vizier proposed the match; for, as he told his Minister plainly, his daughter must not expect to escape the fate which had befallen all the wives who had preceded her.

The Grand Vizier, with tears in his eyes, replied that he and his daughter were well aware of this, but that they would, nevertheless, regard the temporary alliance as a great compliment.

"In that case," said the Sultan, "the marriage can take place tomorrow."

So Sheherazade, gorgeously dressed, was led to the palace. But before she was brought into the presence of the Sultan, she called her sister, Dinarzade, aside and said:

"You know what a good storyteller I am. Well, I shall ask the Sultan to let you lie at the foot of the royal couch, Then, just at daybreak, I want you to beg him to allow me to relate one of my stories for the last time."

Dinarzade willingly agreed to this, and the marriage took place.

Now, as mentioned before, Sheherazade was extremely beautiful, and the Sultan was quite charmed with her, and felt almost sorry that he would have to order her to be put to death in the usual way.

Consequently, he willingly consented to allow her to enjoy her sister's company on the last night of her life.

The day was just beginning to break when, according to arrangement, Dinarzade raised her voice and said:

"Oh! my sister, I wonder if His Imperial Highness would allow you to relate one of your delightful stories. Never shall I hear anything so good again. Do implore him to let me hear one more tale from your lips before they are closed forever."

"What is that?" asked the Sultan sleepily. "Let her tell a story? Why, certainly."

At first he did not pay very much attention to the tale. But, as it went on, he became so enthralled that he felt he simply *must* hear the end. So, as it was time for him to rise and attend to affairs of state, he decided to put off the execution of Sheherazade for another twenty-four hours, or more if required.

The story of "Ali Baba and the Forty Thieves", and others that follow, were the tales told by Sheherazade during the "thousand and one nights," for, as we shall see, each successive night brought a story as wonderful as those that had gone before, and the Sultan eventually fell in love with the fair storyteller, and did not have the heart to kill her. And everyone will agree that, had he done so, he would have been not only a very wicked man, but a very foolish one, too.

ALI BABA AND THE FORTY THIEVES

n a certain town of Persia there lived two brothers, one named Cassim, the other Ali Baba. Cassim had married a wife who brought him a good deal of property, and he had thus become one of the richest merchants in the town.

Ali Baba, on the other hand, had married for love, not for money, and had to eke out his slender means by cutting wood in the forest and selling it in the town. He carried it on three donkeys, which were his only possession.

One day, Ali Baba went to the forest, and had very nearly finished cutting as much wood as his donkeys could carry, when he perceived a thick cloud of dust advancing toward him.

Ali Baba was a cautious man, so he climbed a tree which grew at the foot of a large rock and hid himself among the branches, where he could see without being seen.

Soon a band of horsemen appeared. Ali Baba counted forty, all well-armed and mounted. Each of them tethered his horse and took off the saddle bags, which seemed extremely heavy. Then one, whom Ali Baba took to be the captain, came to the rock and exclaimed: "OPEN, SESAME!" (Sesame is the small seed often used in Persian food).

Immediately a door opened in the rock and they all passed through. The captain went last and the door closed behind them.

The robbers stayed inside the rock for some time, so Ali Baba was compelled to remain in the tree and wait with patience for their departure. He was afraid to leave his place of refuge in case some of them should come out and discover him.

At last the door opened and the forty robbers came out. The captain this time made his appearance first. After he had seen all his troop pass out before him, he exclaimed loud and clear: "SHUT, SESAME!" and the door closed with a clang. Each man then returned to his horse, put on its bridle, fastened his bag and mounted. When the captain saw that they were all ready, he put himself at their head, and they departed on the road by which they had come.

Ali Baba watched till he could see them no longer, and, to be sure of his safety, delayed his descent for a considerable time. He recollected the words the captain of the robbers had used to open and shut the door, and he was curious to see if the door would open if he said them. He therefore made his way through the bushes to the door they concealed, and, said clearly: "OPEN, SESAME!" The door instantly flew wide open.

Ali Baba, who had expected to find only a dark and gloomy cave, was astonished to see a large, spacious, well-lighted and vaulted room, dug out of rock. It was so high that he could not touch the roof with his hand. It received light from an opening at the top of the rock. He discovered a large quantity of provisions, numerous bales of rich merchandise, a store of silk stuffs and brocades, and, besides all this, great quantities of money, both silver and gold, partly piled up in heaps and partly stored in large leather bags placed one on top of another.

Ali Baba did not hesitate a moment, but entered the cave. As soon as he was in, the door closed behind him. But, as he knew the magic words by which to open it, this did not worry him. He paid no attention to the silver, but made directly for the gold coins, and particularly that portion which was in the bags. Having collected as much as he thought he could carry, he went in search of his donkeys, which he had left to look after themselves when he climbed the tree. They had strayed some way, but he brought them close to the door of the rock and loaded them with the sacks of gold, which he then completely covered with twigs. When he had finished his task he pronounced the words: "SHUT SESAME!" The door instantly closed, for, although it shut of itself every time he went in, it remained open on his coming out till he commanded it to close.

Ali Baba now returned to the town and when he got to his own house, drove his donkeys into the small courtyard belonging to it and shut the gate with great care. He then carried the bags into his house and emptied their contents in front of his wife, who was first of all struck speechless, and then accused her husband of having turned robber. But her alarm turned to joy when Ali Baba related his wonderful adventure.

She tried to count the money, but Ali Baba, who was anxious to dig a hole and bury his treasure before any prying eye could see it, declared it would take too long.

"Very well," she said, "dig your hole, and while you are digging it, I will go and borrow a measure from my sister-in-law; for I am determined to know how much money there is."

So, having promised not to breathe a word about the gold, the wife of Ali Baba set off, and went to her brother-in-law, Cassim, who lived a short distance from her house. Cassim was not at home, so she addressed herself to his wife, whom she begged to lend her a small measure for a few minutes.

"With pleasure," said the sister-in-law; "wait a moment and I will bring it to you." She went to bring it; but, knowing the poverty of Ali Baba, she was curious to know what sort of grain his wife wanted to measure. She bethought herself, therefore, of putting some candle wax under the measure, in such a way that it would not be noticed.

The wife of Ali Baba returned home, and, placing the measure on the heap of gold, filled and emptied it till she had measured the whole. Her husband having by this time dug the pit to hold it, she informed him how much it amounted to, and both rejoiced at the greatness of the treasure. While Ali Baba was burying the gold, his wife carried back the measure to her sister-in-law, without noticing that a piece of gold had stuck to the bottom. "Here, sister," said she, "you see I have not kept your measure long. I am much obliged to you for lending it to me."

As soon as the wife of Ali Baba had gone, her sister-in-law examined the bottom of the measure and was most astonished to see a piece of gold sticking to it.

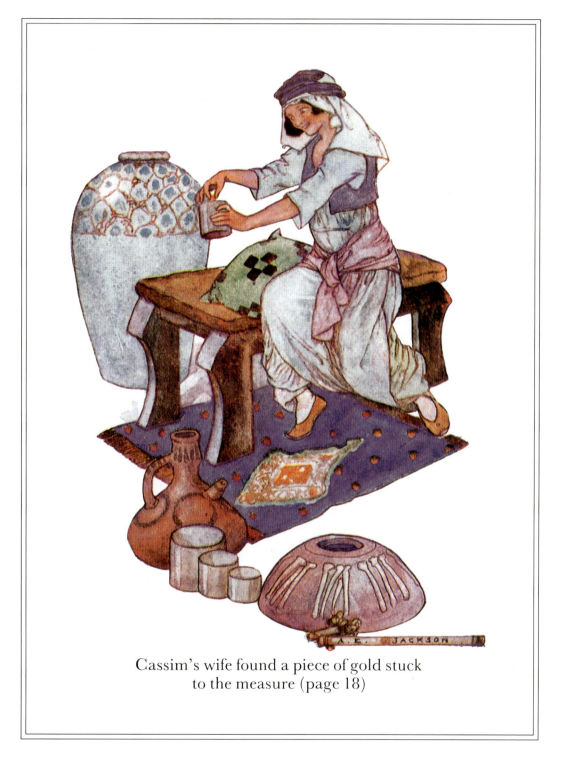

Cassim's wife found a piece of gold stuck
to the measure (page 18)

The frightened Cassim could not remember
the magic word (page 23)

"What!" she exclaimed, "does Ali Baba have such an abundance of gold that he measures instead of counting it? If so, how in the world did he come by it?"

The moment her husband, Cassim, entered the house, his wife flew to him and nearly shouted as she said:

"Cassim, you think you are rich, but Ali Baba has infinitely more wealth: he does not count his money as you do, he measures it." Cassim demanded an explanation, and his wife showed him the piece of money she had found sticking to the bottom of the measure.

Far from feeling any pleasure at his brother's good fortune, Cassim felt extremely jealous. The next morning, before sunrise, he went to Ali Baba with the intention of solving the mystery of this new wealth.

"O, Ali Baba," said he, "you are very reserved in your affairs. You pretend to be poor, and yet you have so much money that you must measure it."

"O, my brother," replied Ali Baba, "I do not understand. Pray explain yourself."

"Do not pretend ignorance," answered Cassim, and, showing Ali Baba the piece of gold his wife had given him, he continued: "How many pieces have you like this, which my wife found sticking to the bottom of the measure that your wife borrowed from her yesterday?"

When Ali Baba found that, thanks to his wife, his sudden wealth was no longer a secret, he told Cassim by what chance he had found out about the thieves' treasure, and he offered, if Cassim would agree to keep the secret, to share the riches with him.

"This I certainly expect you to do," replied Cassim in a haughty tone; and he added: "but I also demand to know the precise spot where this treasure lies concealed, and the signs which may enable me to visit the place myself. If you refuse this information, I will go and inform the police, and you will not only be unable to help yourself to any more money, but also you will lose what you have already taken. On the other hand, I will receive my portion for having informed against you."

Moved more by natural goodness of heart than fear of his brother's threats, Ali Baba gave him the information he demanded, telling him the words he must pronounce both on entering the cave and on leaving it.

Next morning, before break of day, Cassim, full of hope of possessing himself of the entire treasure, set off with ten mules furnished with large hampers which he proposed to fill. He took the road Ali Baba had pointed out, arrived at the rock, and saw the tree, which, from the description, he knew to be the one that had concealed his brother. He soon discovered the door, and pronounced the mystic words: "OPEN SESAME!" The door opened, he entered, and it immediately closed behind him. On examining the cave, he found even more wealth than he expected.

Having feasted his eyes, he started to collect as much treasure as his ten mules could carry. But when, dragging a number of sacks behind him, he came to the door, he found to his great dismay that he had forgotten the right words. "OPEN, BARLEY!" he said, but the door did not budge an inch. He then named the various other kinds of grain, missing the right one, so the door did not move.

At this, fear took possession of his mind. The more he tried to remember the word, the more he failed. He threw the sacks he had collected to the ground and paced backward and forward in a perfect frenzy of terror. The riches which surrounded him no longer had any attraction at all.

Toward noon, the robbers returned to their cave, and when they saw the mules belonging to Cassim standing near the rock, laden with hampers, they were greatly surprised. They all, including the captain, alighted and, drawing their swords, went towards the door and pronounced the magic words which caused it to open.

Cassim, who from inside the cave had heard the trampling of horses, felt sure the robbers had arrived, and that his death was certain. Resolved, however, to make one effort to escape, he posted himself near the door, ready to run out as soon as it opened. The word *sesame*, which he had in vain tried to recall, was scarcely pronounced when the portal opened, and he rushed out with such violence that he knocked the captain to the ground. He could not, however, avoid the other thieves, who cut him to pieces on the spot.

On entering the cave, the robbers at once discovered the sacks of gold which Cassim had left near the entrance, and put them back in place, but they did not notice the absence of those taken by Ali Baba. They were, however, much puzzled as to the means by which Cassim had managed to enter the cave, and, in order to scare off anyone else who might dare enter, they cut the body of the unfortunate Cassim into quarters, and placed them near the door.

Then they mounted their horses and set off to commit more robberies.

The wife of Cassim, in the meantime, began to feel very uneasy as night approached and her husband did not return. She went, in the utmost alarm, to Ali Baba, and said: "O brother, I believe you are well aware that my husband went to the forest, and why he went. He has not yet come back, and I fear some accident may have befallen him."

Ali Baba had suspected his brother's intention after the conversation he had held with him. However, he replied that she need not feel any uneasiness, as Cassim most probably thought it wiser not to return until dark. Thus he soothed her alarm so that she returned to her house and waited patiently till midnight, but after that hour her fears returned with two-fold strength. She spent the night in watching and weeping and at break of day ran to Ali Baba and entreated him to go and look for Cassim.

After advising the distressed wife to restrain her grief, Ali Baba immediately set off with his three donkeys to the forest. As he drew near the rock, he was astonished to see that blood had been shed near the door, and, not having met either his brother or the ten mules on his way, he looked on this as a very bad sign. He reached the rock, and on his pronouncing the magic words, the door opened and he entered. He was struck with horror by the discovery of the body of his brother cut into four quarters. Without losing time in bewailing his fate, he picked up the remains, which he placed on one of his donkeys and covered it with twigs. The other two animals he quickly loaded with sacks of gold, covering them with more twigs. Then, commanding the door to close, he took the road to the city, taking care to wait at the entrance of the forest until dark that he might return without being observed.

When he got home he left the two donkeys that were laden with gold in the care of his wife, and, after telling her what had happened to Cassim, he led the third animal to his sister-in-law's house.

Ali Baba knocked at the door, which was opened to him by a female slave named Morgiana. This Morgiana was very sharp and clever, and Ali Baba knew her abilities well. He broke the bad news to her, and then bade her summon her mistress, who came to him in great anxiety. Ali Baba first made her promise to listen calmly to the story he had to tell, and then related all that had happened.

"Sister," added he, "here is a great and sudden affliction for you, but you must control your grief and do your crying later for we must contrive to bury my brother as though he had died a natural death. I have an idea which, I think, with the help of Morgiana, can be carried out."

At this, the widow of Cassim allowed her sobs to subside, for she was not without common sense, and listened while Ali Baba coached Morgiana in the part she was to play.

Accordingly, Morgiana, who was as sharp as a needle, assumed a woeful expression and went to the shop of the nearest apothecary, where she asked for a particular medicine which was supposed to cure the most serious ailments.

On the following day, Morgiana again went to the apothecary, and, with tears in her eyes, inquired for an essence which it was customary only to administer when the patient was reduced to the last extremity, and when no other remedy had been left untried. "Alas!" cried she, as she received it from the hands of the apothecary, "I fear this remedy will be of no more use than the other and I shall soon lose my beloved master!"

Moreover, as Ali Baba and his wife were seen going to and from the house of Cassim in the course of the day, with very long faces, no one was surprised when, toward evening, the piercing cries of the widow and Morgiana announced the death of Cassim.

At a very early hour the next morning, Morgiana, knowing that an old cobbler who lived some distance off was one of the first to open his shop, went to visit him. Coming up to him, she wished him good day, and put a piece of gold in his hand.

Baba Mustapha, a man well-known throughout the city, was naturally of an amusing turn of mind, and always had something funny to say. He examined the piece of money, and seeing that it was gold, said: "This is a good wage; now what is to be done? I am ready to do your bidding."

"Baba Mustapha," said Morgiana to him, "take all your materials for sewing and come with me; but I insist on this condition, that you let me put a bandage over your eyes when we have reached a certain place."

At these words Baba Mustapha began to make objections. "Oh, ho!" said he, "you want me to do something against my conscience or my good name."

But Morgiana interrupted him by putting another piece of gold in his hand. "Allah forbid," she said, "that I should require you to do anything that would hurt your conscience or stain your name. Just come with me and fear nothing."

Baba Mustapha allowed himself to be led by Morgiana, who bound a handkerchief over his eyes, and brought him to Cassim's house; she did not remove the bandage until he was in the chamber where the remains were placed. Then, taking off the covering, she said: "Baba Mustapha, I have brought you hither that you may sew these four quarters together. Lose no time; and when you have done I will give you another piece of gold."

When Baba Mustapha had finished his gruesome task, Morgiana bound his eyes again, and after giving him the third piece of money, according to her promise, and earnestly requesting him to keep her secret, she conducted him to the place where she had first put on the handkerchief. Here she took the bandage from his eyes and left him to return to his house, watching him, however, until he was out of sight, in case he should decide to return and watch her own movements.

Then the body of the unfortunate Cassim was washed, perfumed, wrapped in an elegant shroud, and buried with due ceremony.

The widow remained at home to lament and weep with the women of the quarter, who, according to custom, had gone to her house during the ceremony, but Morgiana followed the coffin, weeping and tearing her hair.

Ali Baba had a son who had served his apprenticeship with a merchant of good repute. He now placed the young man in charge of the shop which had belonged to Cassim, while he moved with his belongings to his late brother's house, which was larger than his own.

Leaving Ali Baba to enjoy his good fortune, we will now return to the forty thieves. On going back to the cave they were amazed and alarmed to find the body of Cassim gone, together with a large portion of their treasure.

"We have been discovered," said the captain, "and if we are not very careful we shall lose all the riches we have amassed with so much trouble and fatigue. All we know is that the thief whom we surprised when he was going to make his escape knew the secret of the door. But evidently he was not the only one; another must have the same knowledge. And, as we have no reason to suppose that more than two people are acquainted with the secret, having destroyed one, we must not let the other escape. What say you, my brave comrades?"

The other thirty-nine robbers agreed that it would be advisable to give up every other enterprise and occupy themselves solely with this affair until they had succeeded.

"Then," resumed the captain, "the first thing to be done is that one of you who is bold, courageous and cunning, should go to the city, unarmed and in the dress of a stranger, and employ all his art to discover if the singular death we inflicted on the culprit we destroyed is being talked about. Then he must find out who this man was and where he lived. But, in order to prevent his bringing us a false report, which might occasion our total ruin, I propose that the one selected to perform the task shall consent to the penalty of death in case of failure."

Without waiting till his companions spoke, one of the robbers said: "I agree to those terms. If I should fail, you will, at least, remember that I displayed both courage and readiness in my offer to serve the troop."

Amid the commendations of the captain and his companions, the robber disguised himself in such a way that no one could have suspected him of being what he was. He set off at night, and entering the city just as day was dawning, went towards the public bazaar. There he saw only one hop open, and that was the shop of Baba Mustapha.

The merry cobbler was seated on his stool ready to begin work. The robber went up to him and wished him a good morning, saying: "My good man, you rise early to your work; how is it possible that an old man like you can see cl   at this early hour? Even if it were broad day, I doubt whether your eyes are good enough to see the stitches you are making."

"Whoever you are," replied Baba Mustapha, "you do not know much about me. Old as I am, I have excellent eyes; and you would have admitted as much had you known that not long ago I sewed up a dead body as neatly as possible in a place where there was no more light than we have here."

The robber was greatly elated at discovering this important clue so soon. "A dead body!" replied he with feigned astonishment, to induce the other to proceed. "Why should you want to sew up a dead body? I suppose you mean that you sewed the shroud in which he was buried," "No, no," said Baba Mustapha, "nothing of the kind. But, anyhow, it is no business of yours."

Upon this, the robber produced a piece of gold, and putting it into Baba Mustapha's hand, said; "Keep your temper and your secret, too, if you like. All the same, if you would care to earn this piece of money, you can do so by showing me the house where you performed this extraordinary piece of needlework."

"Should I feel inclined to grant your request," replied Baba Mustapha, holding the piece of money in his hand as if ready to return it, "I assure you I could not do it, for the simple reason that I was securely blindfolded both coming and going."

"But at least," resumed the robber, "you must have some idea of the way you went after your eyes were bound. Pray, come with me. I will put a bandage over your eyes at the place where you were blindfolded, and we will walk together along the same streets, and follow the same turnings, which you will probably remember having taken; and, as all work deserves a reward, here is another piece of gold."

The two pieces of gold were a great temptation to Baba Mustapha.

"Well, well," he said, "I will do my best " He then conducted the robber to the spot where Morgiana had put the bandage over his eyes. "This is the place," said he, "where my eyes were bound, and then my face was turned in this direction." The robber, who had his handkerchief ready, tied it over the old man's eyes and walked by his side, partly leading him, and partly led by him, till Baba Mustapha stopped.

"I think I did not go farther than this." He was, in fact, exactly in front of the house which had once belonged to Cassim, and where Ali Baba now resided. Before taking the bandage from the cobbler's eyes, the robber quickly made a mark on the door with some chalk he had brought for the purpose and, when he had taken the handkerchief off, he asked Baba Mustapha if he knew to whom the house belonged. The cobbler replied that he did not live in that quarter of the town, and therefore could not tell. Whereupon, the robber thanked him, and, when he had seen the cobbler set out for his shop, took the road to the forest, where he felt sure his tidings would be welcome.

Soon after the robber and Baba Mustapha had separated, Morgiana had occasion to go out on some errand; and when she returned she observed the mark which the robber had made on the door of the house. "What can this mean?" she thought. "Has anyone a spite against my master, or has it been made only for diversion? Anyhow, I will take precautions." She therefore found a piece of chalk, and as several of the doors on each side of Ali Baba's house were of the same appearance, she marked them in the same manner.

In the meantime, the thief quickly made his way back to the forest, where he rejoined his companions and related the success of his journey. After some discussion, it was arranged that the spy should return to the city, accompanied by the captain, and make further investigations.

But, when the two arrived at the house where Ali Baba lived, they were confronted by a whole row of doors with chalk marks, though the robber declared, with an oath, that he had marked but one.

The captain was much annoyed, but there was nothing for it but to return to the forest, where the unlucky robber had his head cut off as the penalty for his failure.

In spite of this, another robber, who flattered himself with hopes of better success, requested to be allowed to see what he could do. Permission being granted, he went to the city, bribed Baba Mustapha with more gold, and the cobbler, with his eyes bound, went through the same performance and led him to the house of Ali Baba.

The thief marked the door with red chalk in a place where it would be less noticed, thinking this would be a surer method of distinguishing it. But, a short time afterwards, Morgiana went out, as on the preceding day, and the red mark did not escape her sharp eyes. She immediately made a similar mark on all the doors nearby.

When he returned to his companions in the forest, the thief boasted of the precautions he had taken to distinguish the house of Ali Baba, to which he offered to lead the captain without fail. But the result was the same. A whole row of front doors marked with red chalk met the captain's irritated eye and the second robber lost his head.

This reduced the forty thieves to thirty-eight and the captain determined to undertake the task himself. He therefore went to the city and, with the assistance of Baba Mustapha, found the house of Ali Baba but, having no faith in chalk marks, he imprinted the place thoroughly on his memory, looking at it so attentively that he was certain he could not mistake it.

He then returned to the forest, and when he reached the cave said, "Comrades, I now know with certainty the house of the culprit who is to experience our revenge and I have planned a first-rate way of dealing with him."

He then charged them to divide into small parties and go into the nearby towns and villages and there buy nineteen mules and thirty-eight large leathern jars for carrying oil. One extra jar must be full, and all the others empty.

In the course of two or three days, the thieves had completed their purchases to the captain's satisfaction. He made each one of the men, thoroughly armed, enter each jar. He then closed the jars so that they appeared to be full of oil, leaving, however, a

Ali Baba quickly loaded his asses with
sacks of gold (page 26)

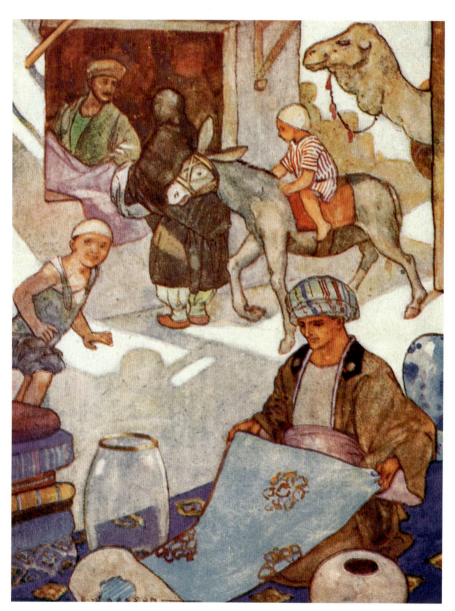

The robber captain opened a shop
opposite Ali Baba's (page 46)

sufficient space to admit air for the men to breathe and, the better to carry out the deception, he rubbed the outside of each jar with oil, which he took from the full one.

Thus prepared, the mules were laden with thirty-eight robbers, each concealed in a jar, along with the jar that was filled with oil. Then the captain, disguised as an oil merchant, took the road to the city, where the whole procession arrived about an hour after sunset. The captain went straight to the house of Ali Baba, intending to knock and request shelter for the night for himself and his mules.

However, he was spared the trouble of knocking, for Ali Baba was at the door, enjoying the fresh air after supper. He stopped his mules and addressing himself to Ali Baba, said: "My good friend, I have brought the oil which you see here from a great distance to sell tomorrow in the market; and at this late hour I do not know where to obtain shelter for the night. If it would not cause you much inconvenience, do me th kindness to take me in and I shall be greatly obliged."

Although Ali Baba had seen the man in the forest who now spoke to him, and had even heard his voice, he did not know him in his excellent disguise.

"You are welcome," he said, and immediately

made room for the visitor and his mules to enter. A stable and fodder were made ready for the mules, after which Ali Baba went into the kitchen to tell Morgiana to get supper quickly for a guest who had just arrived, and also to prepare him a chamber and a bed.

The captain of the robbers attempted to excuse himself from accepting the bed, alleging that he was, loath to be troublesome, but in reality that he might have an opportunity of executing his plan with more ease; and it was not until Ali Baba had used the most urgent persuasions that he agreed.

Ali Baba remained with his guest until he saw that he had all he requested. Then he wished him good night and said: "You are at liberty to do as you please. You have only to ask for whatever you want. All I have is at your service."

The captain of the robbers thanked him profusely. Then, while Ali Baba went into the kitchen to speak to Morgiana, he stole away to the stable under the pretext of going to see after his mules.

Ali Baba, having again enjoined Morgiana to be attentive to his guest, added: "Tomorrow before daybreak I shall go to the bath. Take care that my bathing linen is ready, and give it to Abdalla" (this was the name of his male slave) "and make me some broth to eat for I shall be hungry when I return."

After giving these orders, he went to bed.

The captain of the robbers then found his way to the stable and gave his men their orders. Beginning at the first jar, and going from one to another, he said to the armed thief in each: "When I throw some stones from the room where I am to be lodged tonight, do not fail to rip open the jar with the knife I have given you and come out. I shall be with you immediately afterwards."

He then returned and was conducted by Morgiana to the chamber she had prepared for him. Not to create suspicion, he put out the light a short time after, and lay down in his clothes to be ready to rise as soon as he considered it safe to do so.

Morgiana did not forget Ali Baba's orders. She prepared her master's linen for the bath and gave it to Abdalla. Then she put the pot on the fire to make the broth, but while she was skimming it, the lamp went out. There was no more oil in the house and she had no candle, so she did not know what to do. "What are you worrying about?" said Abdalla. "All you have to do is to go and take some oil out of one of the big jars in the stable."

Morgiana thanked Abdalla for the idea, and, while he retired to bed, she took her oil jar and went to the stable. As she drew near the jar that stood first in the row, the thief who was concealed within said in a low voice: "Is it time?"

Any slave but Morgiana would, in the surprise of finding a man in the jar instead of the oil she expected, have jumped and screamed. But Morgiana at once felt the extreme danger in which Ali Baba and his family, as well as herself, were placed. Consequently, she assumed the manner of the captain, and answered: "Not yet, but very soon." She then went on to all the vessels in succession, making the same answer to the same question, till she came to the last jar, which was full of oil.

Morgiana by this discovered that her master had afforded shelter to thirty-eight robbers, including the pretended merchant who was their captain. She quickly filled her vessel from the last jar and returned to the kitchen. Then, having lighted her lamp, she took a very large kettle and went again to the stable to fill it with oil from the jar. This kettle she immediately put upon the fire, for she had a plan for the preservation of the family which required the utmost speed. As soon as the oil boiled, she took the great kettle and, returned to the stable, poured into each jar, from the first to the last, sufficient boiling oil to stifle and destroy the robber within.

When Morgiana had performed this brave act, she returned to the kitchen, blew out the lamp and waited to see what would happen.

She had scarcely waited a quarter of an hour when the captain of the robbers awoke. He got up, opened the window and gave the signal agreed upon. He listened, but heard nothing. After a while, overcome by uneasiness, he stole from his chamber and made his way to the stable. On approaching the first jar, he detected a strong scent of hot oil. He proceeded to the next jar, and to all in succession, and discovered that all his men had shared the same fate. He knew his plan to revenge himself by the destruction of Ali Baba and all his household had failed, and the sooner he made his own escape, the better.

When Morgiana saw that the captain of the thieves did not return, she rightly concluded that he had escaped through the garden. Consequently, she retired to rest, feeling very pleased with herself.

When Ali Baba returned from the bath early next morning, he was met at the door by Morgiana, who, with an air of mystery, led him to the stable and, pointed to one of the oil jars, begged him to look inside.

He did as she desired, and, perceiving a man in the jar, uttered a cry of surprise. "Morgiana!" he exclaimed, "tell me immediately what does this mean?"

"Look first in all the other jars," she replied.

When Ali Baba had done so, and found a dead robber in each, Morgiana told him the events of the preceding night: how she had discovered and killed the thirty-eight thieves, and how the captain of the band had escaped.

She also informed him of the mysterious chalk marks on the door, and of the manner in which she had made them useless.

When she had finished her tale, Ali Baba, with deep emotion, observed: "You are no longer my slave, but my benefactress. I give you your liberty from this moment, and will soon reward you in more ample manner. I am convinced that the captain of the robbers laid this snare for me and, through your means, Allah has delivered me. What we have now to do is to use the utmost speed in burying the bodies, which we must do with secrecy, and, for this purpose, I will instantly go to work with Abdalla."

Ali Baba's garden was of considerable size, and ended in a clump of large trees. He went with his slave without delay to dig a ditch, or grave, under these trees, of sufficient size to contain the bodies. They then took the bodies out of the jars and placed them in the grave. After this, Ali Baba carefully concealed the oil jars. As for the mules, he sent them to the market at different times, and disposed of them by means of the slave.

Meanwhile, the captain of the forty thieves had returned to the forest in a condition of rage and despair, which gradually gave way to a determination to make a final effort to avenge himself upon Ali Baba, whom he held responsible for the destruction of the entire band. Therefore, the very next day, having assumed a fresh disguise, he returned to the city, where he took lodgings at an inn. He supposed that the events which had happened in the house of Ali Baba would have become generally known, so he asked the host for any news of the town. In reply to him, the host talked on a variety of subjects, but never mentioned the one the captain had nearest at heart. By this the latter concluded that the reason Ali Baba kept the transaction secret was that he did not wish to divulge the fact that he had access to so immense a treasure.

To carry out his plan, the captain provided himself with a horse, which he made use of to convey to his lodgings several kinds of rich stuffs and fine linens, bringing them from the cave in the forest at various times. In order to dispose of this merchandise he decided to open a store. Having found one that suited him, he stocked it with his goods and established himself in it. The shop, as it happened, was exactly opposite the one that had belonged to Cassim, and was now occupied by the son of Ali Baba.

The captain of the robbers, who now assumed the name of Cogia Houssain, took an early opportunity of getting on friendly terms with the shopkeepers nearby. The son of Ali Baba, being young and of a pleasing manner, and the captain making a point of talking with him more than with others, soon led the two into close friendship. This apparent friendship grew even more quickly when the captain discovered that the young man was the son of his enemy, Ali Baba.

The son of Ali Baba did not like to receive treats and hospitality from his new friend without making some return. On mentioning this to his father, Ali Baba willingly undertook to provide an entertainment. "My son," said he, "tomorrow is Friday, when most of the merchants close their shops. I will give orders to Morgiana to prepare a supper to which you shall invite your new friend, Cogia Houssain."

Though the former captain of the forty thieves by this means got his way by gaining admission to the house of his enemy, he was most anxious not to take a meal beneath his roof. Therefore, though he entered the house and received a hearty welcome from Ali Baba, he tried to leave before supper, giving as a reason his dislike to eat of any dish that contained salt. But Ali Baba hospitably refused to accept any excuse. "If that is your only reason," he said, "it need not deprive me of the pleasure of your company. In the first place, the bread which is eaten in my house does not contain salt; and as for the meat and other dishes, I promise you there shall be none in those which are placed before you. I will now go to give orders to that effect."

Ali Baba went into the kitchen and told Morgiana not to put any salt in the meat she was going to serve for supper. He also told her to prepare two or three other dishes he had ordered without any salt.

Morgiana could not refrain from expressing some surprise at this new order. "Who," said she, "is this man who eats no salt with his meat? Your supper will be spoiled if I have to suit his whims."

"Do not be angry," replied Ali Baba. "He is an honest man; do as I tell you."

Morgiana obeyed, though much against her will. She felt a great curiosity to see this man who did not eat salt. So when she had finished her preparations, and Abdalla had prepared the table, she helped to

TALES FROM THE ARABIAN NIGHTS

carry in the dishes. On looking at Cogia Houssain, she knew him at once, notwithstanding his disguise, as the captain of the robbers, and she also perceived that he had a dagger concealed under his robe.

"I am not surprised," said she to herself, "that this villain will not eat salt with my master. He is his bitterest enemy and means to murder him, but I will prevent him."

When Morgiana had finished bringing in the dishes and assisting Abdalla to wait upon the company, she left the room in order to carry out a purpose she had in her mind, leaving Ali Baba, his son, and their guest to enjoy their wine and dessert.

Cogia Houssain, or rather the former captain of the forty thieves, now thought he had a good opportunity. "I will make them both drunk," thought he, "and then the son will be unable to prevent me plunging my dagger in the heart of his father and I shall escape by way of the garden, as I did before, while the cook and the other slave are at their supper, or, perhaps, asleep in the kitchen."

But, instead of going to supper, Morgiana dressed herself like a dancing girl and stuck a dagger in her girdle. Then she said to Abdalla, "Take your tambourine and let us go and entertain our master's guest, who is the friend of his son, by the music and

48

dance we sometimes perform together."

Abdalla took his tambourine and accompanied Morgiana to the supper chamber. She then begged her master to allow her to do something to entertain his guest. "A capital idea," observed Ali Baba approvingly.

And, though Cogia Houssain would gladly have dispensed with this diversion, he, too, pretended to be highly pleased.

So Abdalla played the tambourine with all the skill he could command, and Morgiana danced. After she had performed several dances with great grace and agility, Morgiana drew out the dagger and began to flourish it as though this were a part of the performance – sometimes pretending to stab the air, and sometimes herself.

At length, apparently out of breath, she took the tambourine from Abdalla with her left hand and, holding the dagger in her right, presented the tambourine, with the hollow part upward to Ali Baba, in imitation of the professional dancers, who were accustomed in this way to appeal to spectators for money.

Ali Baba threw a piece of gold into the tambourine. Morgiana then presented it to his son, who followed his father's example. Cogia Houssain had already taken a piece of money from his purse when Morgiana, with a courage and promptness equal to the resolution she had formed, plunged the dagger in his heart.

Ali Baba and his son, terrified at this action, uttered a loud cry.

"Wretch!" exclaimed Ali Baba, "what hast thou done? Thou hast ruined me and my family forever."

"What I have done," replied Morgiana, "is not for your ruin, but for your safety." Then, opening Cogia Houssain's robe to show Ali Baba the dagger which was concealed under it, she continued: "Behold the cruel enemy you had to deal with! Look at his face attentively, and you will see the disguised oil merchant and the captain of the forty robbers. Do you not recollect that he refused to eat salt with you? From the moment you told me of this, I suspected him. Are you not convinced that my suspicions were well founded?"

Ali Baba, who now understood the fresh obligation he owed to Morgiana for having thus preserved his life a second time, kissed her on both cheeks and said: "Morgiana, I gave you your freedom, and, at the same time, promised to show you stronger proofs of my gratitude at some future period. This period has now arrived I present you to my son as his wife."

Then, addressing his son, he continued: "I believe you to be too dutiful a son to take it amiss if I bestow Morgiana upon you without previously consulting your inclinations. Your obligation to her is not less than mine."

Far from showing any discontent, Ali Baba's son replied that he willingly consented to the marriage, not only to prove his ready obedience to his father's wishes, but because his own inclination prompted him to do so.

They then resolved to bury the captain of the robbers by the side of his former companions; and this duty was performed with such secrecy that the circumstance was not known till many years had passed, and no one was any longer interested in keeping this memorable history concealed.

A few days after the burial, Ali Baba ordered the nuptials of his son and Morgiana to be celebrated. He gave a sumptuous feast to which he invited all his friends and neighbours, and if the guests felt any surprise at the match, they took care not to show it.

Ali Baba, who had not revisited the cave since he had brought away the body of his brother lest he should meet with any of the thieves and be slain by them, still refrained from going there even after the death of the thirty-eight robbers and their captain because he was ignorant of the fate of the other two, and supposed them to be still alive and looking for him.

At the expiration of a year, however, finding that no attempt had been made to disturb his peace, he had the curiosity to make a journey to the ave. He mounted his horse and when he approached the cave, seeing no trace or either men or horses, he thought this a good omen. He dismounted, and fastening his horse, went to the door and said the words: "OPEN SESAME!" The door opened and he entered.

The state in which everything appeared in the cave led him to judge that no one had been in it from the time when the disguised Cogia Houssain had opened his shop in the city. He therefore concluded that the whole troop of robbers was totally dispersed or exterminated; that he himself was now the only person in the world who was acquainted with the secret of entering the cave, and that consequently the immense treasure it contained was entirely at his disposal. He had provided himself with a bag, and filled it with as much gold as his horse could carry, with which he returned to the city.

So Ali Baba and his son, whom he took to the cave and taught the secret of entering, lived happily ever after; and their descendants, who were also entrusted with the secret, lived in great contentment, enjoying their riches with moderation, and gaining the highest offices of the city.

SINDBAD THE SAILOR

In the reign of the Caliph Haroun Alraschid, there lived in Baghdad a poor porter named Hindbad. One day, during the violent heat of summer, he was carrying a heavy load from one end of the city to the other, when he came to a street where the pavement was sprinkled with rose water, before a large mansion. From its windows came not only sounds of melody but also delicious smells of cooking, which to Hindbad seemed a hundred times better. A grand feast was in progress, he concluded, and he felt some curiosity to know who was the fortunate person to whom the house belonged. He therefore ventured to put the question to some handsomely dressed servants who were standing at the door.

"What!" was the reply, "are you an inhabitant of Baghdad and do not know that this is the residence of Sindbad the sailor, that famous voyager, who has roamed over all the seas under the sun?"

The porter, who had heard of the immense riches

Hindbad was invited into the mansion by
Sindbad's servant (page 57)

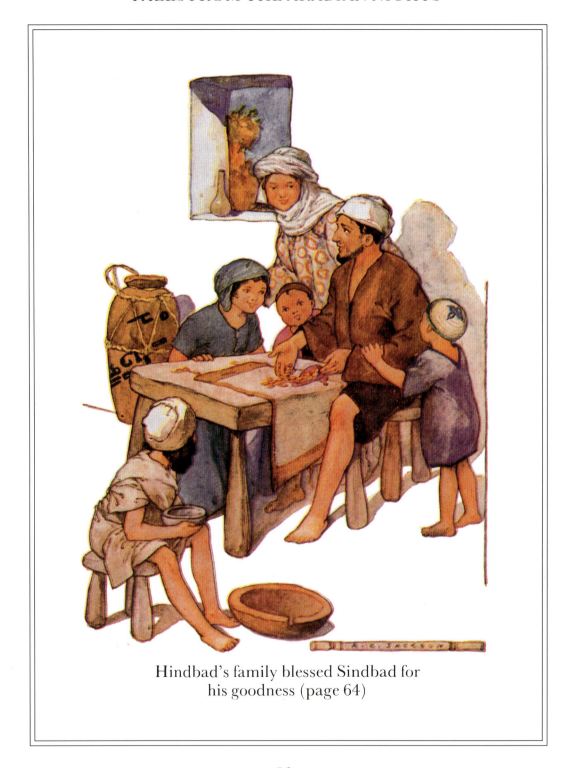

Hindbad's family blessed Sindbad for
his goodness (page 64)

of Sindbad, could not help comparing the situation of this man with his poverty-stricken condition, and exclaimed in a loud voice: "Almighty Creator of all things, deign to consider the difference there is between Sindbad and myself. I suffer daily a thousand ills, and have the greatest difficulty in supplying my family with bad barley bread, while the fortunate Sindbad enjoys every pleasure. What has he done to obtain so happy a destiny, and what crime has been mine to merit a fate so hard?"

He was still musing on this when a servant came toward him from the house and said: "Come, follow me. My master, Sindbad, wishes to speak to you."

Remembering the words he had uttered, Hindbad feared that Sindbad intended to reprimand him, and therefore tried to excuse himself by declaring that he could not leave his load in the middle of the street. But the servant assured him that it would be taken care of, and pressed him so much that the porter could not very well refuse.

His conductor led him into a spacious room where a number of people were seated round a table, which was covered with all kinds of luxuries. In the principal seat sat a grave and venerable personage, whose long white beard hung down to his breast. This person was Sindbad, to whom the porter made obeisance with fear and trembling. Sindbad told him to approach, and to his surprise and embarrassment, seated him at his right hand and helped him to the choicest dishes and the finest wine.

Toward the end of the repast, Sindbad inquired the name and profession of his guest.

"Sir," replied the surprised porter, "my name is Hindbad."

"I am happy to see you," said Sindbad, "and I would like you to repeat the words I overheard you utter a little while ago in the street."

At this Hindbad hung his head and replied: "Sir, I must admit that I uttered some indiscreet words, which I entreat you to pardon."

"Oh," resumed Sindbad, "do not imagine I am so unjust as to have any resentment on that account, but I must undeceive you on one point. You appear to suppose that the riches and comforts I enjoy have been obtained without work or trouble. You are mistaken. Before attaining my present position, I endured the greatest mental and bodily sufferings you can possibly imagine. Perhaps you have heard only a confused account of my adventures in the seven voyages I have made, and as an opportunity now offers, I will relate to you and the rest of this company some of the dangers I have encountered.

Listen, then, to the history of my first voyage."

THE FIRST VOYAGE

I squandered the greater part of the fortune I inherited from my father in youthful dissipation, but at length I saw my folly and resolved to collect the small remains of my inheritance and employ it profitably in trade. This I did, and then went to Basra, where I embarked with several merchants in a vessel which had been equipped at our joint expense.

We set sail and steered toward the Indies by the Persian Gulf touching at several islands, where we sold or exchanged our merchandise. One day, we were unexpectedly becalmed before a little green island which was of a most attractive appearance. The captain gave permission to go ashore to those passengers who wanted to, and of this number I was one. But, while we were enjoying ourselves, the island suddenly trembled and we felt a severe shock.

Those who had remained in the ship immediately called to us to get back on board or we would perish, for what we supposed to be an island was really the back of a huge whale. The most active of the party jumped into the boat, while others dived into the water to swim to the ship. As for me, I was still on the island, or, more properly speaking, on the whale, when it dived below the surface, and I had only time to seize a piece of wood which had been brought to make a fire with, when the monster disappeared beneath the waves. Meanwhile, the captain, anxious to take advantage of a fair breeze which had sprung up, set sail with those who had reached his vessel and left me to the mercy of the waves. I remained in this deplorable situation the whole of that day and the following night. On the second morning, I had neither strength nor hope left, but when I was at my last gasp, a breaker happily threw me onto an island.

Much weakened by fatigue, I crept about in search of some herb or fruit that might satisfy my hunger. I found some, and also had the good luck to discover a stream of excellent water. Feeling much stronger, I began to explore the island and entered a beautiful plain, where I perceived some fine horses grazing. While I was admiring them, a man appeared who asked me who I was. I related my adventure to him, whereupon he led me into a cave. There I found some other people, who were not less astonished to see me than I was to meet them.

I ate some food which they offered me, and upon my asking them what they did there, they replied that they were grooms to the King of that island, and the horses were brought there once a year for the sake of the excellent pasturage. They told me that tomorrow was the day fixed for their departure, and if I had been one day later I must certainly have perished because they lived so far off that it would have been impossible for me to have found my way without a guide.

The following day they returned with the horses to the capital of the island, whither I accompanied them. On our arrival the King, to whom I related my story, gave orders that I should be taken care of and supplied with everything I might want.

As I was a merchant, I associated with people of my own profession in the hope of meeting someone with whom I could return to Baghdad, for the capital of the island is situated on the sea coast, and has a beautiful port, where vessels from all parts of the world arrive daily.

As I was standing near the port one day, I saw a ship come toward the land. When the crew had cast anchor, they began to unload its goods. Happening to cast my eyes on some of the packages, I saw my name written thereon, and knew them to be the ones which I had loaded on the ship in which I left Basra. I also recognized the captain, and asked him to whom those parcels belonged.

"I had on board with me," replied he, "a merchant of Baghdad, named Sindbad. One day, when we were near an island, or at least what appeared to be one, he went ashore with some other passengers. But this supposed island was nothing but an enormous whale that had fallen asleep on the surface of the water. The monster no sooner felt the heat of a fire they lighted on its back to cook their meal, than it began to move and flounce around in the sea. Most of the persons who were on it were drowned, and the unfortunate Sindbad was one of the number. These parcels belonge to him, and I have resolved to sell them so if I should meet any of his family, I may be able to pay over to them the profit I shall have made."

"Captain," said I then, "I am that Sindbad whom you supposed dead, but who is still alive, and these parcels are my property."

When the captain heard me speak thus he exclaimed: "That is impossible. With my own eyes I saw Sindbad perish; the passengers I had on board were also witnesses of his death. And now you have the nerve to say that *you* are that same Sindbad? At first sight you appeared a man of probity and virtue, yet you are not above telling an outrageous falsehood in order to possess yourself of merchandise which, quite obviously, does not belong to you."

"Have patience," replied I, "and listen to what I have to say."

I then related in what manner I had been saved, and by what lucky accident I found myself in this part of the country.

The captain was rather staggered at first, but was soon convinced that I was not an impostor. Then, embracing me, he exclaimed: "Heaven be praised that you have escaped. Here are your goods. Take them by every right."

I thanked him, and selected the most precious and valuable things in my bales as presents for the King, to whom I related the manner in which I had recovered my property. He accepted the presents and gave me others of far greater value. Thereupon I took my leave, and again embarked on the same vessel in which I had first set out, having first exchanged what merchandise remained for aloes, sandalwood, camphor, nutmegs, cloves, pepper, ginger, and other products of the country. We touched at several islands, and at last landed at Basra, from whence I came to Baghdad. And, as I had made about a hundred thousand gold pieces as the result of my voyage, I determined to forget the hardships I had endured and to enjoy the pleasures of life.

Having thus concluded the story of his first voyage, Sindbad ordered a purse containing a hundred gold pieces to be brought to him and gave it to the porter, saying: "Take this, Hindbad: Return to your home and come again tomorrow to hear the continuation of my history."

The porter returned home and the account he gave of his adventure to his wife and family made them call down many blessings on the head of Sindbad.

On the following day, Hindbad dressed himself in his best clothes and went again to the house of Sindbad, who received him in a friendly manner. As soon as the guests had all arrived the feast was served, and when it was over, Sindbad said: "My friends, I will now give you an account of my second voyage."

THE SECOND VOYAGE

As I told you yesterday, I had resolved to pass the rest of my days in peace in Baghdad. But the desire to travel returned, so I bought some goods and set sail with other merchants to seek my fortune.

We went from island to island, bartering our goods very profitably. One day, we landed on one which was covered with a variety of fruit trees, but we could not discover any habitation or the trace of a human being. While some of my companions were amusing themselves by gathering fruits and flowers, I seated myself under some trees and fell asleep. I cannot say how long I slept, but when I rose to look for my companions, they were all gone, and I could only just see the vessel in full sail, at such a distance that I soon lost sight of it.

After some moments given to despair, I climbed a high tree to look about me, and, gazing around on land and sea, my eye was caught by a large white spot in the distance. I climbed down quickly, and, making my way towards the object, found it to be a ball of prodigious size. When I got near enough to touch it, I found it was soft and so smooth that any attempt to climb it would have been fruitless. Its circumference might have been about fifty paces.

The sun was then near setting, and suddenly it seemed to be obscured as by a cloud. I was surprised at this change, but how much did my amazement increase, when I perceived it to be occasioned by a bird of most extraordinary size, which was flying towards me. I recollected having heard sailors speak of a bird called a roc, and I concluded that the great white ball which had drawn my attention must be the egg of this bird. I was not mistaken, for shortly afterwards the bird alighted on the white ball and seated itself upon it. When I saw this huge fowl coming, I drew near to the egg so that I had one of the claws of the bird just in front of me; this claw was as big as the trunk of a large tree. I tied myself to the claw with the linen of my turban, in hopes that the roc, when it took flight the next morning, would carry me with it away from that desert island. My project succeeded, for at break of day the roc flew away, and bore me to such a height that I could no longer see the earth. Then it descended with such rapidity that I almost lost my senses. When the roc had alighted, I quickly untied the knot that bound me to its foot, and had scarcely released myself when it darted on a serpent of immeasurable length, and seizing the snake in its beak, flew away.

The place in which the roc left me was a very deep valley, surrounded on all sides by mountains of such height that their summits were lost in the clouds, and so steep that there was no possibility of climbing them.

As I walked along this valley, I noticed that it was strewn with diamonds, some of which were of astonishing size. I amused myself for some time by examining them, but soon perceived from afar some objects which destroyed my pleasure, and created great fear in me. These were a great number of enormous serpents. To escape from them, I retired into a cave, the entrance of which I closed with a stone, and there I ate what remained of the provisions I had brought from the ship.

All night long I could hear the terrible hissing of the serpents, which retired to their lairs at sunrise. Then I left my cave with trembling, and may truly say that I walked a long time on diamonds without feeling the least desire to possess them. At last, I sat down and fell asleep, for I had not once closed my eyes during the previous night. I had scarcely begun to doze when the noise of something falling awoke me. It was a large piece of fresh meat and at the same moment I saw a number of other pieces rolling down the rocks from above.

I had never believed the accounts I had heard from seamen and others of the Valley of Diamonds, and of the means by which merchants procured these precious gems. I now know it to be true. The method is this: the merchants go to the mountains which surround the valley, cut large pieces of meat and throw them down, and the diamonds on which the lumps of meat fall stick to them. The eagles, which are larger and stronger in that country than in any other, seize these pieces of meat to carry to their young at the top of the rocks. The merchants then run to the eagles' nests, force the birds to go away, and then take the diamonds that have stuck to the pieces of meat.

I had begun to look on this valley as my tomb, but now felt a little hope. I therefore collected the largest diamonds I could find, and with these filled the leather bag in which I had carried my provisions. I then took one of the largest pieces of meat, tied it tightly around me with my turban, and laid myself on the ground.

I had not been in this position long before the eagles began to descend, and each seized a piece of meat with which it flew away. One of the strongest darted on the piece to which I was attached, and carried me up with it to its nest. The merchants then began their cries to frighten away the eagles; and when they had obliged the birds to quit their prey, one of them approached but was much surprised and alarmed on seeing me. He soon, however, recovered from his fear and began to quarrel with me for trespassing on what he called his property.

"You will speak to me with pity instead of anger," said I, "when you learn by what means I reached this place. Console yourself, for I have diamonds for you as well as for myself, and my diamonds are more valuable than those of all the other merchants put together."

Saying this, I showed him my store. I had scarcely finished speaking when the other merchants, perceived me and flocked round with great astonishment; their wonder was still greater when I related my history and showed my diamonds, which they declared to be much greater in size and quality.

As all were now contented with their share of the diamonds which I distributed among them, we set out next day, going over high mountains which were infested by large serpents, which we had the good fortune to escape. We reached the nearest port, where I exchanged some of my diamonds for valuable merchandise; and at last, after having touched at several ports, we reached Basra, from which place I returned to Baghdad.

Here Sindbad came to the end of his second voyage. He again ordered a hundred pieces of gold to be given to Hindbad, whom he invited to come the next day. As before when the repast ended, he began to tell the story of his third voyage.

THE THIRD VOYAGE

I soon forgot the dangers I had encountered in my two voyages, and, tired of doing nothing, again set sail with merchandise from Basra for parts unknown.

After a long voyage, during which we touched at several ports, we were overtaken by a violent tempest, which made us lose our way. The storm continued for several days and drove us near an island where we were forced to cast anchor, in spite of the fact that it was inhabited by a very savage race of dwarfs. Their number was so great that the captain warned us to make no resistance, or they would pour upon us like locusts and destroy us. This information, which alarmed us very much, proved only too true; for very soon we saw advancing a multitude of frightening beings, entirely covered with red hair and about two feet high. They threw themselves into the sea, swam to the ship and soon came swarming on the deck.

Unfurling the sails, they cut the cable, and after dragging the ship ashore, forced us to disembark.

We left the shore, and, penetrating into the island, found some fruits and herbs, which we ate in fear and trembling. As we walked, we perceived a large building in the distance, towards which we bent our steps. It was a lofty palace with folding gates of ebony, which opened as we pushed them. We entered the courtyard and saw, facing us, a vast apartment with a vestibule. On one side of this was a large heap of human bones and on the opposite side appeared a number of spits for roasting.

The sun was setting, and while we were still stunned with horror, the door of the apartment suddenly opened with a loud noise and there entered a frightening-looking man who was as tall as a large palm tree. In the middle of his forehead gleamed a single eye, red and fiery as a burning coal; his front teeth were long and sharp and projected from his mouth, which was as wide as that of a horse; his ears resembled those of an elephant and covered his shoulders, and his long nails were curved like the talons of an immense bird.

At this sight, we almost lost our senses, and when, after closely examining us, he seized me and began to pinch me all over, I felt that I was as good as dead. Fortunately, he found me too skinny. So, dropping me, he seized the captain, who was the fattest of the party, and, using one of the spits roasted him like a sparrow and ate him for his supper. He then went to sleep, snoring louder than thunder.

He did not wake till the next morning, but we passed the night in the most terrible suspense. When daylight returned, the giant awoke and went out, leaving us in the palace.

We sought to escape, but could find no way.

Towards evening the giant returned and supped upon another of my unfortunate companions. He then slept, snored, and departed at daybreak, as before.

Our situation was so hopeless that some were on the point of throwing themselves into the sea. But I dissuaded them, as I had a plan which I proceeded to impart to them.

"My friends," said I, "you know that there is a great deal of wood on the seashore. Let us get some rafts in readiness and then take the first opportunity of executing the plan I have thought of." My advice was approved by all, and we immediately built some rafts, each large enough to support three persons. These rafts we carefully concealed.

On the giant's return, another of our party was sacrificed. But we were soon revenged on him for his cruelty. As soon as we heard him snore, I and nine of the most courageous among us, each took a spit, and making the points red hot, thrust them into his eye and blinded him.

The pain made him groan hideously. He threw his arms around on all sides to try and catch us, but we were able to avoid him. At last he found the door, and went out, bellowing with pain. We at once ran to the shore where our rafts lay, but were obliged to wait until daybreak before embarking.

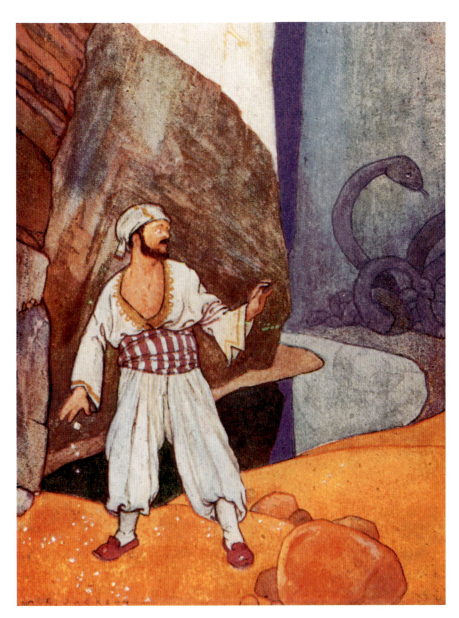

The bird left Sindbad in a valley
full of serpents (page 67)

Sindbad waved his turban to attract
attention (page 76)

The sun had scarcely risen, however, when, to our horror, we saw our cruel enemy, led by two giants nearly as huge as himself, and accompanied by several others coming towards us, obviously ready to seek revenge.

We immediately ran to our rafts and rowed away as fast as possible. The giants, seeing this, picked up some huge stones, and, wading into the sea to their waists, hurled them at the rafts, and sank all but the one I was on. Thus, I and two companions were the only men who escaped.

We rowed with all our strength and were soon beyond reach of the stones and gained the open sea, where we were tossed about for a day and a night. We then had the good fortune to be thrown on an island, where we found some excellent fruit. This soon restored our strength and courage.

When night came on, we went to sleep on the seashore, but were soon awakened by the noise made by the hissing of an immense serpent, which devoured one of my companions before he had time to escape.

My other comrade and myself took flight, during which we noticed a very high tree. This we climbed, hoping to spend the night there in safety. The hissing of the serpent again warned us of its approach, and, twining itself round the trunk, it swallowed my unfortunate companion, who was on a lower branch than myself and then went away.

I remained on the tree till daybreak, and then descended, more dead than alive.

However, towards evening, I collected a great quantity of wood and furze, and, tying it in bundles, placed it in a circle round the tree. Then, tying another bundle upon my head, I sat down within the circle. The serpent returned with the intention of devouring me, but, though he watched and waited the whole night, he was prevented from approaching me by the rampart I had formed. He retired at sunrise, but I felt that death would be preferable to such another night of horror, and so ran towards the sea. But, as I was about to cast myself in, I saw a ship at a distance. I cried out with all my strength, and unfolded and waved my turban to attract the attention of those on board. It did so, and the captain sent a boat to rescue me.

All on board were amazed at the story of my narrow escape, and treated me with the greatest kindness and generosity.

One day, the captain called me and said: "Brother, I have in my possession some goods which belonged to a merchant who was a passenger on my ship. As he is dead, I am going to have them valued, that I may render an account of them to the heirs of this man, whose name was Sindbad. In this task I shall be glad of your assistance."

At this, I looked at the captain in amazement, and knew him to be the one who, on my second voyage, had left me asleep on the island.

We were both of us changed in appearance, which accounted for neither at first knowing the other. But, on my declaring myself, he remembered me, and begged my forgiveness for the error by which I had been abandoned. "God be praised for your escape," cried he. "Here are your goods, which I have preserved with care, and now have the greatest pleasure in restoring to you."

And so, with all this additional wealth, I landed at Basra again, and came from there to Baghdad.

Sindbad thus finished the story of his third voyage. Again he gave Hindbad a hundred gold pieces, inviting him to the usual repast on the morrow, when he continued the story of his adventures.

THE FOURTH VOYAGE

In spite of the terrible dangers I had encountered on my third voyage, it was not long before I tired of the land, and again set sail with merchandise.

All went well until one day we met with a sudden squall and were driven on to a sandbank, where the boat went to pieces and a number of the crew perished.

I and some others had the good fortune to get hold of a plank, on which we drifted to an island. There we found fruit and fresh water with which we refreshed ourselves and then lay down to sleep and regain our strength.

The next morning, when the sun had risen, we left the shore and walking inland, saw some dwellings towards which we made our way.

But they proved to be inhabited by a number of ferocious people, who took us prisoners and made all but myself eat of a certain herb.

I refused, as I had a presentiment of some evil purpose; and I was right, for my companions shortly became light-headed and did not know what they said or did.

Then a meal of rice cooked in coconut oil was offered us, of which I ate very sparingly, but which the others devoured ravenously. This rice was to fatten us, for we had the terrible misfortune to have fallen into the hands of cannibals, who intended to feast on us when we were in good condition.

And so, one by one, my poor companions, who had

lost their senses and could not foresee their fate, were devoured. On the other hand I, who ate next to nothing, daily became thinner and less palatable.

In the meantime, I was allowed a great deal of liberty, and one day took the opportunity to escape. I walked for seven days, taking care to avoid those places which appeared to be inhabited, and living on coconuts, which afforded me both drink and food.

On the eighth day I came to the seashore, where I saw some people employed in gathering pepper, which grew very plentifully in that place, and who, as soon as I approached them, asked me in Arabic where I came from.

Delighted to hear my native language once more, I readily satisfied their curiosity; and when they embarked I went with them to the island from which they had come. I was presented to their King, who was astonished at the story of my adventures. He took a liking to me and treated me with such kindness that I almost forgot my previous bad luck.

I noticed one thing which appeared to me very singular: everyone, the King not excepted, rode on horseback without saddle, bridle, or stirrups. I one day took the liberty to ask his Majesty why such things were not used in his city. He replied that he had never heard of the articles of which I spoke.

I immediately went to a workman and gave him a model from which to make the tree of a saddle. When he had executed his task, I myself covered the saddle tree with leather, richly embroidered in gold, and stuffed it with hair. I then went to a locksmith, who made me a bit and some stirrups according to the patterns I gave him.

These things I presented to the King, who was highly delighted with them, and, as a sign of his pleasure, bestowed upon me, as a wife, a lady, beautiful, rich and accomplished. I lived happily with her for some time, though I often thought regretfully of my native city of Baghdad, and longed to return there.

One day, the wife of one of my friends, with whom I was very close, fell sick and died. I went to console the widower, and, finding him in the deepest depression, said to him: "May God preserve you, and grant you a long life."

"Alas!" replied he, "I have only one hour to live. This very day, according to the custom of the country, I shall be buried with my wife."

While I was still mute with horror at this barbarous custom, his relatives and friends came to make arrangements for the funeral. They dressed the corpse of the woman as though she were a bride and decorated her with jewels; then they placed her on an open bier, and the procession set out. The husband, dressed in mourning, went next, and the relatives followed.

They made their way to a high mountain, on the summit of which was a deep pit covered with a large stone; into this the body was lowered. The husband, to whom a jug of water and seven small loaves were given, then took leave of his friends and allowed himself to be lowered into the pit, and the stone was replaced.

I was much affected by this and expressed my horror to the King. "What can I do, Sindbad?" he replied. "It is a law common to all ranks, and even I submit to it. I shall be interred alive with the Queen, my consort, if she happens to die first."

"And must strangers submit to this cruel custom?" I asked.

"Certainly," said the King, "they are not exempt when they marry on the island."

After this, you may imagine my distress when my wife died after a few days' illness. I almost regretted that I had not been eaten by the cannibals, and though the funeral procession was graced by the presence of the King and his whole court, I was not in the least consoled, and followed the body of my wife, deploring my miserable destiny. At the last moment I tried to save my life by pleading my position as a stranger, but in vain. I was lowered into the pit with my seven loaves and a jug of water, and the opening was covered by the stone.

In spite of the horror of my situation, I lived for some days on my provisions. But one day, when they were exhausted and I was preparing to die of starvation, I heard a sound of loud breathing, together with footsteps. I felt my way in that direction and saw a shadow which fled before me. I pursued it until, at last, I perceived a small speck of light resembling a star, and kept on toward it till I arrived at an opening in the rock, through which I scrambled and found myself on the seashore. Then I discovered that the object I had followed was a small animal which lived among the rocks.

I cannot describe my joy at this escape. But, after a time, I ventured to return to the cave and collect a great quantity of jewels and gold ornaments, which had been buried with the dead. These I hid and then returned to the shore in time to see a ship approaching.

I managed to attract attention by shouting and waving my turban. I was taken on board, and at length arrived once more in safety at Baghdad.

Sindbad here concluded the story of his fourth voyage. He repeated his present of a hundred gold coins to Hindbad, whom he requested, with the rest of the company, to return on the following day, when he began the account of his fifth voyage.

THE FIFTH VOYAGE

It was not long before the peaceful and pleasant life I led pallet on me. This time, I built a vessel of my own, on which I took several other merchants as passengers, and we set sail with a fair wind and a rich cargo. The first place we stopped at was a desert island, where we found the egg of a roc as large as that of which I spoke on a former occasion. It contained a small roc, almost hatched, for its beak had begun to pierce the shell. My companions, in spite of my advice, broke open the egg with hatchets, and roasted the young bird, bit by bit.

They had scarcely finished their meal when two immense clouds appeared in the air at a considerable distance. The captain cried out that the father and mother of the young roc were coming, and warned us to get on board as quickly as possible to escape the danger which threatened us. We took his advice, and set sail immediately.

The two rocs approached, uttering the most terrible screams, which they redoubled on finding their egg broken and their young one destroyed. They then flew away toward the mountains whence they had come, and we hoped we had seen the last of them.

But they soon returned, each with an enormous piece of rock in its claws, which, when they were directly over our ship, they let fall. Our ship was smashed, and all on board either crushed to death or drowned except for me.

I was under water for some time, but, coming to the surface, was able to seize a piece of wreckage. With the aid of this, I reached an island on which I landed with some difficulty.

When I had rested awhile, I proceeded farther inland and was charmed by the beauty of all I saw. I ate of the ripe fruits which hung from the trees on every side and drank from the crystal streams.

When night came I lay down to rest on a mossy bank, and when the sun rose I continued on my way until I came to a little rivulet, beside which I saw an old man seated.

I greeted him, and asked what he was doing there; but, instead of answering, he made signs to me to take him on my shoulders and cross the brook, making me understand that he wanted to gather some fruit that grew on the other side.

Accordingly, taking him on my back I waded through the stream. When I had reached the other side, I stooped for him to alight. Instead, he clambered onto my shoulders, crossed his legs round my neck and gripped me so tightly round the throat that I was nearly strangled. I fell to the ground.

But he still kept his place on my shoulders and kicked me so hard that I was forced to rise. He then made me walk under some trees, the fruit of which he gathered and ate. He never loosened his hold during the day or night, always clinging to my neck.

From this time forward, I was his beast of burden. All attempts to dislodge him were in vain until, one day, I chanced to find several dried gourds, which had fallen to the ground from the tree where they had grown. I took a large one, and, after having cleaned it out, into it I squeezed the juice of several bunches of grapes, which the island produced in great abundance. This I left in a particular spot for some days until I found the juice converted into wine.

I drank some of it, and it had such an exhilarating effect that, in spite of my burden, I began to dance and sing. Noticing this, the old man indicated that he also wished to taste the liquor, which he liked so well that he emptied the gourd. The wine went almost immediately to his head, and he began to sway to and fro on my shoulders. Before long his grasp relaxed and I was able to throw him to the ground, where I killed him with a blow from a big stone.

I was much rejoiced at getting rid of this old man, and set out toward the seashore. There I met some people who were travelling on a vessel which had anchored there to get fresh water. They were much astonished at seeing me and hearing the account of my adventure.

"You had fallen," said they, "into the hands of the Old Man of the Sea, and you are the first of his captives whom he has not strangled sooner or later. On that account, the sailors and merchants who land here dare to do so only in a strong body."

They then took me with them to their ship, and in a few days, we anchored in the port of a large city.

One of the merchants on the ship had become very friendly with me. When we landed, he gave me a large sack and then introduced me to some other people who were also furnished with sacks, and said: "Go, follow these people, and do as they do."

We set off together and arrived at a large forest of coconut trees, the trunks of which were so smooth that it was impossible for anyone climb them except the monkeys who lived among the branches.

My companions then collected stones which they threw at the monkeys, who retaliated by hurling coconuts; and, in this way, we easily obtained enough to fill our sacks. By selling these nuts to merchants in the city, I made a handsome profit in the course of time.

I then took passage in a ship which called for a cargo of coconuts. It was bound for the Island of Kamari, which was celebrated for its pearl fishing.

Here I hired divers, and was very fortunate to obtain a number of fine pearls. I again set sail and landed at Basra, having still further increased my riches, a tenth part of which I donated to a charity as was now my custom on returning from a voyage.

At the end of this narrative Sindbad, as usual, gave a hundred pieces of gold to Hindbad, who left with all the other guests. The same party returned the next day, and after their host had regaled them in as sumptuous a manner as on the preceding days, he began the account of his sixth voyage.

THE SIXTH VOYAGE

About a year after my return from my fifth voyage, I again embarked on a ship, the captain of which intended to make a long voyage.

It proved indeed long, for the captain and pilot lost their way, and did not know how to steer. When, at last, the captain discovered our whereabouts, he threw his turban on the deck, tore his beard and beat his head, like a man distraught.

On being asked the reason for this action, he replied: "We are in the greatest peril. A rapid current is hurrying the ship along, and we shall all perish in less than a quarter of an hour. Pray Allah to deliver us from this dreadful danger, for nothing can save us unless He takes pity on us."

He then gave orders to hoist more sail, but the ropes broke in the attempt and the ship became quite unmanageable. It was dashed by the current against a rock, where it split and went to pieces. Nevertheless, we had time to take off our provisions, as well as the most valuable part of the cargo.

When we were assembled on the shore, the captain said: "Allah's will be done. Here we may dig our graves, for we are in a place so desolate that no one cast on this shore has ever returned to his own home from here."

The mountain, at the foot of which we stood, formed part of an island, the coast of which was covered with wreckage and all kinds of valuable merchandise in bales and chests which had been thrown up by the sea. Indeed, if we could have lived on gold or jewels, all might have been well. As it was, starvation was bound to overcome us before very long.

One strange thing in connection with the place was a river of fresh water which ran from the sea and disappeared into a cavern of the mountain.

We remained on the shore in a hopeless condition, for the mountain was too steep to climb and we were thus without any means of escape. And so the fate we feared gradually overcame us. Those who died first were interred by the others. I had the dismal office of burying my last companion, for I had eaten more sparingly of my share of the stock of provisions which had been divided among us, and so held out the longest. Nevertheless, when I buried the last of them, I had so little food left that I imagined I must soon follow him.

But Allah had pity on me and inspired me with the thought of examining the river which lost itself in the recesses of the cave. Having done so, I decided to make a raft and trust myself to the current, and see where it would take me. If I perished, it was but altering the manner of my death.

I set to work at once and made a strong framework of wood bound with rope, of which there was an abundance scattered around the shore. I then selected the chests containing the most valuable jewels and stuffs among the wreckage and when I had carefully stowed all these things so as to balance the raft, I embarked on my vessel, guiding it with a little oar which I had provided, and resigning myself to Providence.

The current carried me under the vault of the cavern. I soon found myself in darkness, and rowed for what appeared to be days, without seeing a single ray of light.

During this time, I consumed the very last of my hoarded stock of provisions. I then either fell asleep or became unconscious. When I regained my senses, I was surprised to find myself in an open country near a river bank, to which my raft had been fastened, and surrounded by a number of strange people.

I felt so overcome with joy that I could scarcely believe myself awake. Being, at length, convinced that my deliverance was not a dream, I gave thanks aloud, on which one person, who could understand Arabic, advanced and said:

"Do not be alarmed at the sight of us. The river which issues from yonder mountain is that from which we get water for our fields. When we saw your

Sindbad presented the splendid saddle
to the King (page 80)

Sindbad loaded the raft with jewels and
valuable goods (page 90)

raft being borne toward us, we swam to it and guided it to shore. And now I beg you to tell us whence you came and what adventures have befallen you."

I replied: "I will do so, with pleasure, when I have eaten, for I am at the point of starvation."

I satisfied my hunger and then proceeded to satisfy their curiosity; afterwards they declared they must take me to their King. So, having procured a horse for me, they hauled my raft ashore and followed me with it on their shoulders to the city of Serendib, where their King received me with great kindness and consideration.

To him I related all that had befallen me and he was so pleased with the history of my adventures that he ordered it to be written in letters of gold and preserved among the archives of his kingdom. The raft was then produced, and, prostrating myself before him I said: "If your Majesty will make me happy by accepting my cargo, the whole is at your disposal."

But, although he smiled and appeared pleased, he refused my offer, saying that, when I left his kingdom, I should take with me proof of his regard.

After I had spent some days examining the city and its surroundings, I begged to be allowed to return to my own country. The King not only gave me permission, together with a gift of great value, but also showed his esteem by entrusting me with a letter and gifts for the Caliph Haroun Alraschid.

These gifts included a vase made of a single ruby, filled with pearls, and a female slave of incredible grace and beauty, who wore jewels worth a King's ransom.

After a long but fortunate voyage, we landed at Basra, whence I returned to Baghdad. I at once executed my commission and presented the letter and the gifts of the King of Serendib to the Caliph, who, after he had put a number of questions to me concerning the country from which I had returned, dismissed me with a handsome present.

Sindbad here finished his discourse, and his visitors left. Hindbad, as usual, received his hundred gold pieces. The guests and the porter returned on the following day, and Sindbad told them about his seventh and last voyage.

THE SEVENTH AND LAST VOYAGE

I now determined, as I was past the prime of life, to go to sea no more, but enjoy a pleasant and restful existence at home.

But one day the Caliph sent for me.

"Sindbad," he said, "I want you to do me a

service. You must go once more to the King of Serendib with my answer and presents, for it is but right that I should make him a proper return for the civility he has shown me."

"Commander of the Faithful," I replied, "I humbly entreat you to consider that I am worn out with the fatigues I have undergone in my six voyages. I have even made a vow never again to leave Baghdad."

I then took occasion to relate the long history of my adventures. When I had finished speaking, the Caliph said: "I confess that these are extraordinary adventures. Nevertheless, they must not prevent you from making the voyage I propose, which is only to the island of Serendib. You must be aware that it would be beneath my dignity if I remained under obligation to the King of that island for any longer than necessary."

As I plainly saw that the Caliph had resolved on my going, I signified that I was ready to obey his commands. At this, he provided me with a thousand pieces of gold to pay the expenses of the voyage.

In a few days, having received the presents from the Caliph, together with a letter written with his own hand, I set off to Basra, where I embarked, I hoped for the last journey, and, after a pleasant voyage, arrived at the faraway island of Serendib.

I soon obtained an audience with the King, who showed pleasure at the sight of me. "Welcome, Sindbad," said he. "I assure you I have often thought of you since your departure. Blessed be this day in which I see you again."

After thanking the King for his kindness, I delivered the letter and presents of the Caliph, which he received with every mark of pleasure.

The Caliph had sent him a complete bed of gold tissue, fifty robes of a very rare stuff, a hundred more of the finest white linen, a bed of crimson velvet, and another of a different pattern and hue. Besides this, he sent a vase of agate, carved in the most wonderful manner.

Soon after this, I requested leave to depart, which the King granted, at the same time giving me a handsome present. I then embarked; but three or four days after we had set sail we were attacked by pirates, who easily made themselves masters of our vessel. Those who attempted resistance lost their lives. I and all those who had the prudence to submit quietly were made slaves. After they had stripped us and clothed us in rags instead of our own garments, the pirates set their course for a distant island, where they sold us.

I was purchased by a rich merchant, who took me home with him. Some days later, he asked me if I could shoot with a bow and arrow.

I replied that I had followed that sport in my youth, and that I did not think I had entirely lost my skill. He then gave me a bow and some arrows, and, making me mount behind him on an elephant, took me to a vast forest some hours' journey from the city. We went deep into the forest, till the merchant came to a particular spot, where he made me dismount. Then he showed me a large tree. "Climb that tree," said he, "and shoot at the elephants that pass under it, for there are many of these animals in this forest. If one should fall, come and let me know."

Thereupon, he left me some provisions and returned to the city.

During the first night no elephants came, but the next day, as soon as the sun had risen, a great number made their appearance. I shot many arrows at them, and at last one fell. The others immediately went, leaving me at liberty to go and inform my master of my success.

He praised me and returned with me. We dug a pit and buried the elephant so that the body might rot and the tusks be more easily obtained.

I continued my new occupation for two months,

and not a day passed in which I did not kill an elephant. But one day, instead of going away as usual, the elephants herded together and came toward me, trumpeting loudly, and in such numbers that the ground trembled under their tread. They approached my tree and surrounded it with their trunks extended, and their eyes all fixed upon me. At this surprising spectacle, I was so unnerved that my bow and arrows fell from my hands.

After the elephants had stared at me for some time, one of the largest twisted his trunk round the body of the tree, tore it up by the roots and threw it on the ground. I fell with the tree, but the animal took me up with his trunk, and placed me on his shoulders, where I lay more dead than alive. The huge beast now put himself at the head of his companions and carried me to a little hill, where he set me down, and then went away with the rest.

After I had waited some time, seeing no other elephants, I arose, and perceived that the hill was entirely covered with bones and tusks of elephants. Evidently, this was their cemetery, and they had brought me hither to show it me, that I might desist from destroying them merely for the sake of possessing their tusks. Realizing the horrible truth about what I had done, I did not stay there long, but turned my steps towards the city, and, after walking for a day and a night, arrived at my master's.

As soon as he saw me, he exclaimed:

"Ah, my poor Sindbad! I have been wondering what could have become of you. I have been to the forest, where I found a tree newly torn up by the roots, and your bow and arrows on the ground. And so I despaired of ever seeing you again. Pray tell me by what fortunate chance you are still alive."

I satisfied his curiosity; and the following day he accompanied me to the hill, and, with great joy, convinced himself of the truth of my story. We loaded the elephant on which we had come with as many tusks as it could carry, and when we returned my master said:

"Brother, I give you your liberty. We have not hitherto been able to get ivory without risking the lives of our slaves. Now our whole city will be enriched by your means, and I shall take care that you are rewarded accordingly."

To this I replied: "The only recompense I desire is permission to return to my own country."

"Well," he replied, "you will have an opportunity shortly, for the monsoon will bring us vessels, which come to be laden with ivory. On one of them you may obtain passage."

The ships at length arrived and my master, having chosen the one in which I was to embark, loaded it with ivory, giving over half the cargo to me, which I ultimately sold for a large sum.

Arriving at Baghdad without any further adventures, I immediately presented myself to the Caliph, who told me that my long absence had occasioned him some uneasiness, which made him the more delighted to see me return in safety.

He bestowed more presents and prestige upon me, after which I retired to my own home in this my native city of Baghdad, which I have not since left and where I hope to end my days.

*   *   *   *   *   *

 *   *   *   *   *

*   *   *   *   *   *

Sindbad thus concluded the recital of his seventh and last voyage, and, addressing himself to Hindbad added: "Well, my friend, have you ever heard of one who has suffered more than I have, or been in so many trying situations? Is it not just that after so many troubles I should enjoy an agreeable and quiet life?"

Hindbad kissed his hand and said: "I must confess that you have encountered frightful perils. You not only deserve a quiet life, but also are worthy of all the riches you possess, since you make so good a use of them!"

Sindbad made sure Hindbad received another hundred pieces of gold, in addition to which, he continued to show so much kindness that Hindbad, who no longer had a need to follow his late calling, had every reason to bless the name of Sindbad the Sailor for the remainder of his days.

ALADDIN AND THE WONDERFUL LAMP

In the capital of one of the richest and most extensive provinces of China lived a poor, hardworking tailor whose name was Mustapha, together with his wife and his only son, Aladdin.

When the youth was old enough to learn a trade, his father took him to his shop, and began to show him how to use his needle. But no sooner was Mustapha's back turned than Aladdin, who was of an idle and careless disposition, was off, and returned no more during the day. His father frequently punished him but Aladdin did not reform, and with great sorrow Mustapha was obliged at last to abandon him to his lazy ways, which he continued until his father's death.

As Aladdin's mother saw that her son would never follow the trade of his father, she shut up Mustapha's shop and sold off all his stock, while Aladdin gave himself completely to idleness.

One day, when he was about fifteen, he was loafing

with his companions in one of the public places. A stranger who was passing stopped and looked attentively at him.

Whether this stranger, who was a powerful magician, thought he saw in the face of Aladdin signs of a disposition well-suited to his purpose is uncertain, but he very cleverly obtained information concerning Aladdin's family, and found out the sort of character and disposition he possessed. After this, he went up to the youngster, and, taking him aside, asked him if his father was not called Mustapha and whether he was not a tailor by trade.

"Yes, sir," replied Aladdin; "but he has been dead a long time."

On hearing this, the magician threw his arms round Aladdin's neck and embraced him, while tears ran from his eyes. "Alas!" he exclaimed, "I am your uncle. Your father was my most excellent brother, whom for years I have longed to meet once more. The news of his death is sad news, indeed."

He then asked Aladdin where his mother lived, and when Aladdin had informed him, the magician gave him a handful of small coins, saying: "My son, go to your mother, make my respects to her, and tell her I will come and see her tomorrow."

Aladdin ran to his mother, highly delighted with

the money that had been given him. "Pray tell me, mother," he cried, as he entered the house, "whether I have an uncle?"

"No, my child," replied she, "you have no uncle, either on your poor father's side or on mine."

"For all that," answered the boy, "I have just seen a man who told me he was my father's brother and my uncle. He even wept and embraced me when I told him of my father's death. And to prove that he spoke the truth," added he, showing the money he had received, "see what he has given me! He bade me also to be sure and give his kindest greeting to you, and to say that he would come and see you tomorrow."

"It is true, my son," replied Aladdin's mother, "that your father once had a brother; but, to the best of my knowledge, he has been dead for a long time."

The next day the magician again accosted Aladdin while he was with three other boys, and, putting two pieces of gold in his hand, said: "Take this to your mother, my boy. Tell her I intend to come and sup with her this evening, and I send this money so that she may purchase what is necessary."

Aladdin carried the two pieces of gold home to his mother, who used them to the best advantage to buy food. When everything was ready, she told Aladdin to go out into the street and look for his uncle. But before the boy could obey, there was a knock. Aladdin instantly opened the door and saw the magician, who had several bottles of wine in his hands to add to the other good things his money had provided.

When the magician had paid his respects to Aladdin's mother, he seated himself, and observed: "Do not be surprised, my good sister, that you have never seen me during the whole time you have been married to my late brother, Mustapha. It is full forty years since I left this country, and since then I have journeyed nearly all over the world."

He then turned to Aladdin and asked: "What is your occupation? Have you learned any trade?"

But his mother answered for him. "Aladdin," she said, "is a very idle boy. His father did all he could to make him learn his business, but could not get him to work, and since his death, Aladdin will learn nothing, but leads an absolutely idle life. Though I pass the whole day in spinning cotton, I can hardly buy bread for us to eat," and she burst into tears.

"This is not right, Aladdin," said the magician. "Dear nephew, you must think of supporting yourself, and working for your bread. If you have any objection to learning a trade, I will procure you a shop, and furnish it. You shall sell the goods, and with the profits that you make you shall buy other merchandise; and in this manner you will pass your life in ease and prosperity. Consult your own inclinations, and tell me honestly what you think of the plan."

This offer greatly flattered the vanity of Aladdin. He therefore admitted to the magician that he thought well of the suggestion.

"Very well," replied the magician, "I will take you tomorrow and have you properly fitted out, and then we will look about for a shop of the description I have named."

Aladdin's mother, who till now had not been convinced that the magician was really the brother of her husband, no longer doubted when she heard of the good he proposed to do her son. She thanked him sincerely for his kind intentions, and during supper charged Aladdin to prove himself worthy of the good fortune in store for him.

The magician returned the next morning, according to his promise. He took Aladdin to a merchant's where ready-made clothes of every description were sold, and made him try on several suits, saying: "Dear nephew, choose what pleases you best."

When Aladdin saw himself handsomely dressed

for the first time in his life, he overwhelmed his uncle with thanks, while his mother was transported with joy. "O, generous relative," she exclaimed. "I thank you from the bottom of my heart for all you have done. May you live many happy years."

"Aladdin," replied the magician, "is not such a bad boy after all. Tomorrow I will call for him, and we will go on a little trip together. I have no doubt that we shall make something good of him.

The next morning Aladdin got up very early in order to be ready to set out the moment his uncle called for him. As soon as he saw the magician coming, he went to inform his mother of the fact. Then he took leave of her and ran to meet his uncle.

The magician received Aladdin in the most affectionate manner. "Come," said he, with a smile, "I will show you some very fine things today." He then led the boy, who had never been outside the city, through a gate, and showed him some magnificent palaces with beautiful gardens, gradually drawing him on and on until they had left the city far behind.

Aladdin, who had never in his life before taken so long a walk, began to feel tired. "Where are we going, my dear uncle?" he asked. "I can see nothing but hills and mountains in front of us."

"Take courage, nephew," replied his scheming uncle. "I want to show you something that far surpasses in magnificence all you have ever seen before."

At length they came to a narrow valley, situated between two mountains of nearly the same height. "We need go no farther," said the magician. "I am now going to strike a light, and in the meantime, you collect all the dry sticks and leaves you can find in order to make a fire."

Aladdin obeyed, and, as soon as the sticks blazed up, the magician threw a magic perfume on them. A thick and dense smoke immediately arose, the ground shook slightly and opened near the spot where they stood. Then a square stone of about a foot and a half across was disclosed, with a brass ring fixed in the middle of it.

Aladdin, dreadfully alarmed, was about to run away when the magician stopped him. "Do not be afraid," he said, "I desire nothing of you but that you obey me implicitly. I must now inform you that under the stone which you see here is concealed a great treasure, which is destined for you and which will one day make you richer than the most powerful monarchs of the earth. But, in order to guarantee success, you must listen to me and execute in every

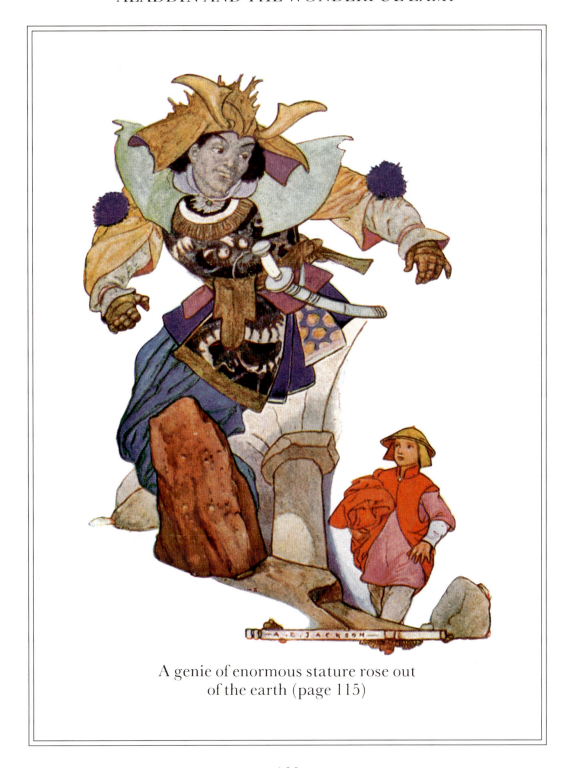

A genie of enormous stature rose out
of the earth (page 115)

Aladdin's mother was astonished at the
sight before her (page 118)

single detail the instructions I am going to give you."

"What must I do?" asked Aladdin, overwhelmed with astonishment at what he had seen and heard. "Tell me. I am ready to obey you in everything."

"I heartily rejoice," replied the magician, "that you have made such a sensible decision. Come, then, take hold of this ring and lift up the stone. It will come up without difficulty."

Aladdin did as the magician told him. Indeed, he raised the stone without any trouble and laid it aside.

When the stone was taken away a hole was visible, at the bottom of which appeared a small door with steps going still lower. "Now, my boy, you must observe exactly every direction I am going to give you. Go down into this cavern, and when you have come to the bottom of the steps, you will see an open door. This leads into three chambers opening out of each other, and each is full of gold and silver. But you must take particular care not to touch any of this treasure. At the end of the third chamber is a door which leads to a garden, planted with beautiful trees, all of which are laden with fruit. Go straight forward and follow a path which you will see, and which will bring you to a flight of fifty steps, at the top of which there is a terrace. When you have ascended to the terrace, you will observe a niche before you, in which there is a lighted lamp. Take the lamp, extinguish it, and bring it to me. If you then want to gather any of the fruit that is grown in the garden you may do so."

Then the magician took off a ring which he had on one of his fingers and put it on Aladdin's hand, telling him that it would guard him against every evil that might happen. "Go," he added, "and descend boldly."

Aladdin jumped into the opening and went down the steps. He found the three chambers and passed through them to the garden. Then, without stopping, he ascended to the terrace. He took the lamp which stood lighted in the niche, extinguished it and put it close to his chest.

On his way back through the garden, he stopped to look more carefully at the fruit, which he had only glanced at before. The fruit of each tree was a different shade. Some were white, other sparkling and transparent; some were red, others green, blue, violet or of a yellowish tint. In short, there were fruits of almost every shade you can name.

The white were pearls; the sparkling and transparent fruits were diamonds; the deep red were rubies; the green emeralds; the blue turquoises; the violet amethysts; those tinged with yellow, amber. All were of the largest size and the most perfect shape ever seen in the world, but Aladdin thought they were only pieces of painted glass. Yet the variety and contrast of so many beautiful shades, as well as the brilliancy and the great size of these fruits, tempted him to gather some of each kind. He took some of every shade, filling all his pockets. He stuffed others in his sash and inside his shirt, until he had no room for more.

Laden in this manner, Aladdin made his way back to the entrance of the cave, where the magician was impatiently waiting. As soon as Aladdin could see him he called out: "Give me your hand, uncle, to help me up."

"My dear boy," replied the magician, "you will do better first to give me the lamp."

"It is not at all in my way," said Aladdin. "I will give it to you when I am out of the cave."

The magician persisted in demanding the lamp before he would help Aladdin out of the cave, but the latter absolutely refused to give it up till he was out. The magician then fell into the most violent rage. He muttered a spell, made some passes with his hands, and the stone which served to shut up the entrance to the cavern returned of its own accord to its place, the earth covering it exactly as when the magician and Aladdin first arrived.

Now the magician, who, of course, was *not* the uncle of Aladdin, had discovered by his magic that there was a wonderful lamp in a cave in the middle of China, the possession of which would make him the most powerful being in the universe if he could succeed in laying hands on it. But it was absolutely necessary that another person should take it and then put it into his hands. For this reason, he had addressed himself to Aladdin, who seemed to be an easily fooled youth well adapted to perform the service; and he had planned, as soon as he took the lamp from the boy, to sacrifice him so that no witness would exist who could say he was in possession of the lamp. But things had not gone the way he expected, and he was in such haste to sacrifice poor Aladdin that he defeated his own object.

When the magician found all his hopes and expectations frustrated, there remained but one thing to do, and that was to return to Africa, his native country. This he did the very same day.

It might be supposed that Aladdin was now hopelessly lost. Indeed, the magician himself, who thought he had destroyed the boy, did not remember the ring he had placed on his finger. Aladdin, who so far did not know the wonderful qualities of either the ring or the lamp, was soon to be enlightened.

When he found himself buried alive, he called aloud a thousand times to his uncle, telling him he was ready to give up the lamp. But all his cries were useless, and, having no other means of making himself heard, he remained in darkness, bemoaning his unhappy fate. Then he descended the steps and groped along the walls to the right and left several times, but could not discover the smallest opening. Finally, he sat down on the steps of his dungeon without the least hope that he would ever again see the light of day.

Aladdin remained in this hopeless state for two days. Then, regarding his death as certain, he lifted his hands, and joining them as in the act of prayer, wholly resigned himself to the will of heaven. In this act of joining his hands he happened to rub the ring which the magician had put on his finger. Instantly, a genie of enormous stature and most horrid appearance rose, as it were, out of the earth before him. This genie was so tall that his head touched the vaulted roof. He said to Aladdin: "What dost thou command? I am ready to obey thee as thy slave, and the slave of all who have the ring that is on thy finger."

On any other occasion, Aladdin would have been struck dumb with terror at sight of this startling figure but he was so taken up with the danger and peril of his situation that he answered without hesitation: "Whoever you are, take me out of this place."

He had scarcely said the words when the earth opened and he found himself outside the cave, at the very spot to which the magician had brought him.

Looking around, he saw the city in the distance. He was so faint and weak that it was *only* with great difficulty that he got home. His mother, who already mourned him as lost or dead, was overcome by joy at the sight of him.

Aladdin begged for food, which he had the sense to eat slowly, while he drank some water with equal moderation. When he had finished he related to his mother all that had happened. He took the lamp out of his jacket and showed it to her, as well as the fruit of jewels that he had gathered as he returned through the garden.

Aladdin had no sooner finished telling of his adventures than his mother began to abuse the imposter of an uncle in the strongest terms. She called him a traitor, an assassin and all the other terrible names she could think of, meanwhile embracing her son and giving thanks for his deliverance.

Aladdin slept soundly all night and, on rising, asked for breakfast. "Alas! my son," replied his mother. "I have not a morsel of bread to give you. Last night you finished all there was in the house. But have patience. I have here a little cotton I have spun. I will go and sell it and purchase something for you to eat."

"Keep that for another time," said Aladdin, "and give me the lamp I brought yesterday. I will go and sell that. The money it will bring will serve us for breakfast and dinner too, nay, perhaps, also for supper."

Aladdin's mother took the lamp from the place where she had placed it. "It seems to me to be very dirty," she said. "I think I will give it a good, hard scrub and then it will surely sell for more."

She then took some water and a little fine sand to clean the lamp; but she had scarcely begun to rub when a hideous and gigantic genie rose out of the ground before her and cried with a voice as loud as thunder: "What are thy commands? I am ready to obey thee as thy slave." The poor woman was so alarmed at this frightening apparition that she fell down in a fit of fainting.

But Aladdin had seen a similar apparition in the cavern and consequently did not lose his presence of mind. He seized the lamp and answered firmly: "Bring me something to eat for breakfast."

The genie disappeared, returning a moment later with a large silver basin, which he carried on his head, and twelve covered dishes of the same material filled with the choicest meats, together with six loaves, two bottles of the best wine, and some silver plates and cups. He placed all these things on the ground and instantly vanished.

All this had occurred so quickly that Aladdin's mother had hardly recovered from her faint before the genie had disappeared for the second time.

On coming to her senses, she was astonished to see the large basin, the twelve dishes, the six loaves, the two bottles of wine, and other things. "O, my son!" she cried, "how did this wonderful spread get here?"

"My good mother," replied Aladdin, "come and sit down and eat. I will tell you everything when we have broken our fast."

When they had made an end of their meal and Aladdin's mother had taken away the things and put aside what had not been consumed, she came and seated herself near her son.

"Why?" she asked, "did the terrible being address himself to me instead of to you, to whom he had appeared in the underground cavern?"

"Mother," replied Aladdin, "the genie who appeared to you just now is not the one who appeared to me. The genie who came to you was the slave of the lamp you had in your hand."

"What!" cried his mother, "was your lamp the reason why this terrible being addressed himself to me rather than to you? Then take it out of my sight. Indeed, I would rather you throw it away or sell it than that I should run the risk of being killed with fright by touching it again. And, if you will follow my advice, you will get rid of the ring as well."

"With your permission, my dear mother," replied Aladdin, "I shall not think of parting with this lamp. Since chance has shown its virtues to us, let us avail ourselves of them. But we must be careful not to make any parade of our new riches lest we draw the envy of others on ourselves. I will take the lamp out of your sight and put it where I shall be able to find it whenever I have occasion for it. Neither do I want nor plan to throw away the ring, but for which you would never have seen me again."

Aladdin's arguments appeared reasonable, so his mother had no further objections to make.

The following morning, Aladdin took one of the silver plates and went out early in order to sell it. He addressed himself to a merchant he happened to meet and, taking him aside, showed him the plate and asked if he would like to buy it.

The merchant took the plate and examined it. As soon as he had satisfied himself that it was good silver, he took out of his purse a piece of gold, which was exactly one seventy-second part of the value of the plate. He offered it to Aladdin, who accepted it eagerly, not knowing its worth.

He and his mother continued to live quietly and economically till Aladdin had sold all the twelve dishes, one after the other. When the money for the last plate was spent, Aladdin took the basin, which was at least ten times as heavy as any of the plates. For this the merchant counted out ten pieces of gold, with which Aladdin was satisfied.

When his ten pieces of gold were spent, Aladdin decided to use the lamp. He took it and rubbed it, and the genie who had appeared before, instantly appeared again. But, as Aladdin had rubbed the lamp more gently than his mother had, the genie spoke to him in a much softer tone.

"What are thy commands?" he asked.

"I am hungry," cried Aladdin. "Bring me something to eat."

The genie disappeared and in a short time returned, loaded as before, and again vanished.

When Aladdin again found his provisions gone, he took one of the new silver dishes and went to look for the merchant who had bought the others from him. As he walked along, he happened to pass the shop of a goldsmith, a respectable and honest old man, who called him into the shop.

"My son," said he. "I have often seen you pass this way, loaded as you are now, and each time you have spoken to a certain merchant. Then I have seen you go back empty-handed. Perhaps you do not know that this person is a great cheat, and that no one who knows him will have any dealings with him. Now, if you will show me what you are carrying to sell, I will faithfully give you what it is worth, if it be in my way of business."

Aladdin was only too pleased to agree to this, whereupon the old man, who knew at a glance that the plate was of the finest silver, took his scales, weighed the dish, and declared it to be worth seventy-two pieces of gold, which he immediately counted out.

Aladdin thanked the goldsmith, and in the future sold his dishes to him and no one else.

Although Aladdin and his mother had an inexhaustible source of money in their lamp, they continued to live with the same frugality they had always shown. Thus, mother and son passed their time happily together for several years with the profitable assistance Aladdin occasionally obtained from the lamp.

During this interval, Aladdin made the acquaintance of some of the most successful merchants of the town and gradually acquired the style and manners of the company he kept. By frequenting the gem shops, he also learned that the fruits he had gathered in the garden, and had taken to be only painted glass, were jewels of enormous value.

One day as he was walking along, Aladdin heard the criers reading a proclamation of the Sultan, ordering the people to shut up their shops and go into their houses until his daughter, the Princess Badroulboudour (a name which means "the full moon among full moons") had passed on her way to the bath and had returned to the palace.

Hearing this order created in Aladdin a curiosity to see the Princess, so he went and hid behind the door of the bath. He had not waited long before the Princess made her appearance, accompanied by a large crowd of women and servants. When she had come within three or four paces of the door, she lifted the veil which had concealed her face, and gave Aladdin the opportunity he desired.

Till this moment, Aladdin had never seen any woman without her veil except his mother, who was rather old, and who, even in her youth, had not possessed great beauty. The appearance of the Princess dispelled the notion he had entertained that all women resembled his mother. She was, in fact, the most exquisite and charming creature imaginable, and it is not surprising that he was absolutely entranced by such loveliness.

When he came home, Aladdin was unable to conceal his state of mind from the observation of his mother. She asked if anything had happened to him, or if he were unwell. He gave her no answer whatever, but continued to brood upon the lovely image of the Princess Badroulboudour.

Aladdin passed a wakeful night, and the next morning he said to his mother: "You may not have heard that the Princess Badroulboudour, the daughter of our Sultan, went to the bath after dinner yesterday. I had the supreme happiness and satisfaction of seeing her, and this, my dear mother, is the true cause of the state you saw me in yesterday, and the reason for the silence I have hitherto kept. I feel such a violent affection for the Princess that I can never know a moment's happiness until she is my own dear wife."

Aladdin's mother listened with great attention till he came to the last sentence. Then she burst into a fit of laughter that echoed round the house.

"Alas! my son," she cried, "you must surely have lost your senses to talk thus."

"Dear mother," replied Aladdin. "I foresaw very well that you would reproach me with folly and madness, but nothing will prevent me from again declaring my resolution to demand the Princess Badroulboudour of the Sultan in marriage."

"In truth, my son," replied his mother, very seriously, "you seem to have forgotten who you are; and even if you are determined to put this resolution into practice, I do not know who will have the boldness to carry your message to the Sultan."

"You yourself must do that," he answered.

"I?" cried his mother in amazement. "I go to the Sultan! Not I, indeed. Nothing will induce me to engage in such an act of folly."

"My dear mother," replied Aladdin, "neither your reasons nor your remonstrances will in the least change my resolution. I have told you that I intend to demand the Princess Badroulboudour in marriage, and that you must impart my wish to the Sultan. I beg you not to refuse me this help."

"My dear son," she replied. "I am your mother

and I am ready to do anything that is reasonable. But, regardless of the lowness of your birth, you demand nothing less than the daughter of the sovereign of this land. Now, suppose I have the impudence to present myself before his majesty and make such a request. Do you not see that I would be treated as a madwoman? And there is another reason, my son. No one ever appears before the Sultan without offering him some gift when a request is made of him. What possible present do you have to offer?"

Aladdin listened with the greatest patience and answered:

"You say it is not customary to request an audience of the Sultan without carrying a present in your hand. I agree with you. But, when you tell me I have nothing worthy of his acceptance, you forget those things we thought were pieces of painted glass. I know their value better now, and can inform you that they are precious stones of priceless value, worthy of the acceptance of a great sovereign."

In the end, Aladdin's mother gave way to her son's arguments. Early the next day, a selection of the jewels having been made and arranged in a porcelain dish, which was then wrapped in a fine linen cloth, she took the road toward the palace of the Sultan.

But, though she succeeded in gaining admission with the rest of the crowd to the Hall of Audience, where the monarch in person heard petitions and administered justice, she returned home without having ventured to approach the Sultan, much to Aladdin's disappointment.

For several days in succession the good woman went to the palace, bearing her offering of jewels, without finding an opportunity of carrying out her mission. On the sixth day, however, the Sultan, on retiring to his apartment, said to his Grand Vizier: "For some time past I have observed a certain woman who comes regularly every day when I hold my council, and who carries something in her hand wrapped in a linen cloth. The next day the council sits and if she returns once more, do not fail to call her so that I may hear what she has to say."

The mother of Aladdin returned to the palace the next day the council met and placed herself opposite the Sultan, who, touched by her patience and perseverance, said to the Grand Vizier, "Do you observe the woman I mentioned to you the other day? Order her to come here, and we will begin by hearing what it is she has to say."

The Grand Vizier immediately pointed out the woman in question to the chief of the ushers, who

The Princess lifted her veil and Aladdin
saw her face (page 122)

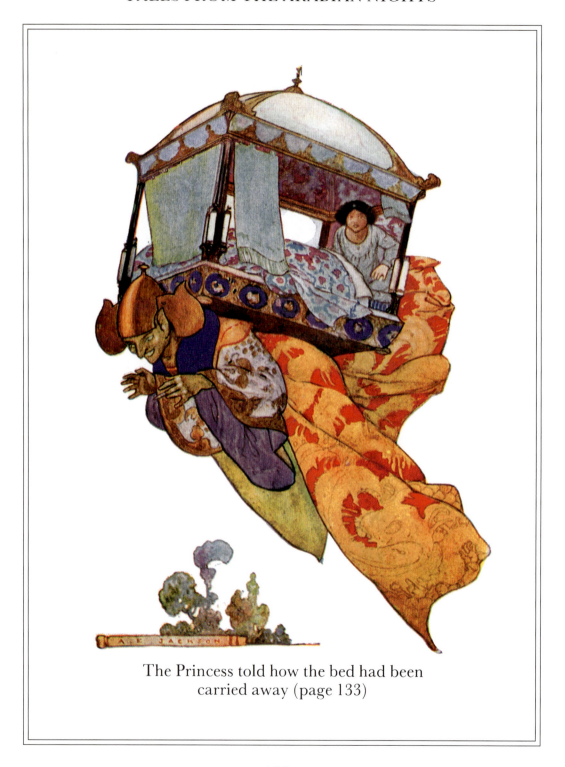

The Princess told how the bed had been
carried away (page 133)

motioned to the mother of Aladdin to approach. She obeyed, and prostrated herself until the Sultan commanded her to rise, saying: "What is the business which brings you here day after day, my good woman?"

Aladdin's mother answered: "Oh, gracious monarch, I entreat you to pardon the boldness of the request I am about to make, which is of a most private nature." The Sultan, having commanded all to withdraw but the Grand Vizier, told her she might speak, and exhorted her to tell the truth without fear.

Aladdin's mother then faithfully related to the Sultan by what means Aladdin had seen the Princess Badroulboudour, and with what a violent passion the sight of the Princess had inspired him, concluding by imploring his pardon for herself and her son, who had dared to dream of so illustrious an alliance.

The Sultan listened to this speech with the greatest patience. Before he made an answer, he asked what it was she had tied up in a cloth. Upon this, Aladdin's mother took up the porcelain dish, which she had set down at the foot of the throne. Removing the linen cloth, she presented the dish to the Sultan.

It is impossible to express the astonishment of the monarch when he beheld such a quantity of the most precious, perfect, and brilliant jewels, greater in size and value than any he had ever seen. After admiring each of the jewels separately, he turned to his Grand Vizier, and said: "What do you say to such a present? Is not the donor worthy of the Princess, my daughter?"

Now the Grand Vizier had entertained great hopes of the Sultan making a match between the Princess and his own son. Therefore he replied:

"Everyone must allow that this present is not unworthy of the Princess. All the same, as the young man is a complete stranger, I beg your majesty to make some excuse to put off the marriage for three months."

The Sultan, who was an easy-going man, agreed to this. "Return home," he said to Aladdin's mother, "and tell your son that I consent to the proposal he has made through you, but the preparations for my daughter's marriage will take three months. At the end of that time, you may return."

As soon as Aladdin saw his mother's face he knew that she had good tidings. And when she had told him all, he thought himself the happiest and most fortunate of mortals, though the three months would seem like three years, he declared.

It happened one evening, when about two months of the time had gone, that Aladdin's mother found she had no oil in the house. Accordingly, she went out to see if she could get some, and on going into the city, perceived signs of great festivity and rejoicing. All the shops were open and decorated with green branches and other ornaments, and preparations were evidently being made for an illumination. Aladdin's mother asked the oil merchant what it all meant. "Where do you come from, good woman," said he, "that you do not know that the son of the Grand Vizier is this very evening to be married to the Princess Badroulboudour?"

Aladdin's mother did not wait to hear more, but returned home with all possible speed.

"All is lost, my son!" she exclaimed. "This very evening the son of the Grand Vizier is to marry the Princess Badroulboudour at the palace."

This news came upon Aladdin like a thunderclap. Then he remembered the power of the lamp, and, retiring to his room, he took it from its hiding place and rubbed it. The genie instantly appeared.

"What are thy commands?" he said to Aladdin.

"Attend to me," answered Aladdin. "I have now a business of great importance for you to undertake. The Sultan promised me the hand of his daughter, but he has, instead, given her in marriage to the son of his Grand Vizier. What I order you to do is this: as soon as the bride and bridegroom have retired to rest, take them up and instantly bring them here."

"Oh, master," replied the genie, "I will obey thee." He immediately disappeared.

In the meantime, every preparation was made in the Sultan's palace to celebrate the nuptials of the Princess, and the whole evening was spent in ceremonies and rejoicings until the time came for retiring.

But the bridegroom had scarcely laid his head upon the pillow when the faithful slave of the lamp took up the bed with the bride and bridegroom still in it, and, to the great astonishment of both, in an instant transported them up into the night sky and across the city to Aladdin's chamber, where he set them down.

Aladdin then ordered him to take the bridegroom and shut him in the lumber room, and to return at daybreak. The genie obeyed. He also improved on Aladdin's orders by breathing on the unfortunate young man and rendering him incapable of move-ment. Then Aladdin addressed himself to the Princess, explaining that what had been done was simply to prevent the Sultan from marrying his daughter to another after he had promised her to Aladdin. But the Princess was so alarmed at this extraordinary adventure that Aladdin could not get a word out of her. So he laid himself down in the place of the Grand Vizier's son, with his back turned toward the Princess, having first placed a drawn sword between the lady and himself.

Punctually the next morning, the genie appeared and, releasing the bridegroom from his uncomfortable position, carried him and the bride back to the palace, the genie in all these operations being visible only to Aladdin.

Both the Sultan and the Sultana visited their daughter in the course of the morning, and were surprised to find her looking very upset. To the inquiries of her father she would answer nothing, but to her mother, the Princess related how, on the previous night, the bed had been taken up and transported to an ill-furnished and dismal chamber, where she was separated from her new husband, whose place was then taken by a complete stranger. Then, when morning approached, her husband was restored to her, and they were both brought back again to the palace in a single instant.

The Sultana listened with great attention, but she could not bring herself to believe her daughter's story.

"You have done well, my child," she said to the

Princess, "not to inform the Sultan, your father, of this matter. Take care that you mention it to no one, unless you wish to be considered a madwoman."

She then ordered the son of the Grand Vizier to be called in order to question him about what the Princess had told her. But the young man felt himself to be in such an embarrassing position that he pretended to be unaware that anything unusual had happened and told her nothing.

The next night at the same time, Aladdin again summoned the genie, with the result that the bride and bridegroom were again whisked off and everything happened precisely as before. But this repetition of her amazing experience so terrified the Princess that, this time, she decided to tell her father, the Sultan, of all that had happened.

The Sultan understood fully the distress this surprising adventure must have excited in his daughter's mind. "My child," said he, "you were wrong not to divulge to me yesterday the strange story you have just related. I have not given you in marriage to make you unhappy. Banish from your memory, then, what you have been telling me. I will take care that you shall experience no more such nights as those which you have suffered."

He then sent for the Grand Vizier, whose son had

also related his alarming and uncomfortable experiences, and who now informed his father that, in spite of the position he derived from his exalted alliance with the daughter of his sovereign, he would rather die than have to undergo any more adventures of that kind. Consequently, when the Sultan spoke to the Grand Vizier of annulling the marriage, he made no objection; and this was, consequently, carried out.

Aladdin, though overjoyed, was not surprised when the news reached him. He allowed the remainder of the three months to elapse, and then again sent his mother to the palace to put the Sultan in mind of his promise. This time she was bolder, and, advancing to the foot of the throne without hesitation, prostrated herself in the usual manner. After she had risen, the Sultan asked her what she wished.

"O, mighty monarch," she replied. "I again present myself before the throne of your majesty to announce to you, in the name of my son Aladdin, that the three months which you said he must wait have expired."

When, on the former occasion, the Sultan had desired a delay of three months before he acceded to the request of this good woman, he thought he would hear no more of a marriage which appeared to him entirely unsuited to the Princess. For, naturally, he judged the suitor's social position from the humble dress and general appearance of his mother.

He therefore consulted in a low tone with the Grand Vizier, who said: "It seems to me that there is a very easy way of avoiding this unequal marriage. It is to set so high a price upon the Princess, your daughter, that all this suitor's riches, however great they may be, cannot come near it."

The Sultan approved of this advice, and, after some little reflection, said to Aladdin's mother: "Good woman, I am ready to make your son happy by uniting him to the Princess, my daughter; but, as I cannot bestow her in marriage till I have seen proof that she will be well provided for, tell your son that I will keep my promise as soon as he sends me forty large basins of precious gold, full of jewels like those you have already presented to me. These basins must be carried by forty black slaves, each of whom shall be accompanied by a white slave, young, handsome, and richly dressed. Go, my good woman, and I will wait till you bring me his answer."

Aladdin's mother again prostrated herself at the foot of the throne and returned home, where she gave her son an exact account of everything the Sultan had said, and of the conditions upon which he would consent to the marriage of his daughter to Aladdin.

Aladdin replied: "What he requires of me is a trifle in comparison with what I would give to possess such a treasure as the Princess. Will you go and prepare dinner and leave me awhile to myself?"

As soon as his mother had gone, Aladdin took the lamp and rubbed it. The genie instantly appeared and demanded to know what was required of him.

"The Sultan agrees to give me the Princess, his daughter, in marriage," said Aladdin, "but he demands of me forty large basins of precious gold, filled with jewels. He requires, also, that these forty basins should be brought to him by forty young and handsome black slaves, accompanied by an equal number of white slaves, richly dressed. Go and get all of this for me as soon as possible."

In a short time, the genie returned with forty black slaves, each carrying upon his head a large golden basin of great weight, full of pearls, diamonds, rubies, and emeralds. They were accompanied by forty white slaves. Aladdin expressed his satisfaction and the genie disappeared.

Aladdin's mother now returned from market, and great was her surprise at the sight which met her eyes. But, before she could speak, she was told she must at once return to the palace and deliver the amazing dowry he had demanded to the Sultan.

As this magnificent procession of black and white slaves all gorgeously arrayed and laden with jewels, passed through the streets, followed by the mother of Aladdin, people came running from all sides.

On the arrival of the slaves at the palace, the porters bowed to the ground, thinking they must be the retinue of some great prince. The Sultan, informed of what was happening, ordered the doors to be thrown open, and the whole party, prostrating themselves in a half circle, placed the jewels on the ground at the foot of the throne, while the mother of Aladdin thus addressed the monarch: "O, mighty ruler, my son, Aladdin, is well aware that the present he has sent your majesty is much beneath the inestimable worth of the Princess Badroulboudour. He, nevertheless, hopes that your majesty will graciously accept it and that it may find appreciation in the eyes of the Princess."

The Sultan hesitated no longer. The mere sight of such immense riches, and the wonderful speed with which Aladdin had fulfilled his exorbitant request without making the least difficulty, persuaded him that Aladdin must be a desirable son-in-law.

"Go, my good woman," he said, his eyes fixed greedily upon all this wealth, "and tell your son I am waiting with open arms to receive and embrace him, and that the greater diligence he uses in coming to receive from my hands the gift I am ready to bestow on him, in the person of my daughter, the greater pleasure he will afford me."

The mother of Aladdin returned home, swelling with pride and happiness. "You have every reason, my dear son," she said, "to be satisfied. The Sultan has announced that you are worthy to possess the Princess Badroulboudour, and he is now waiting to embrace you and to conclude the marriage."

Aladdin was delighted at this intelligence and instantly retired to his chamber. He then took up the lamp, rubbed it, and immediately the genie showed his obedience to its power by appearing in readiness to execute his commands.

"Oh, genie," said Aladdin to him. "I now desire thee to provide me with a richer and more magnificent robe that was ever worn by any monarch."

This was a very simple matter for the genie, and the garment in which he now assisted Aladdin to array himself was so dazzling that it made the eyes of the beholder ache. He also provided him with a horse with a golden harness and saddle studded with gems, and forty more slaves, in addition to ten thousand pieces of gold to distribute to the crowd.

Aladdin's mother was not forgotten, for her dutiful son presented her with six magnificent dresses and as many female attendants.

Aladdin then mounted his horse and began his triumphal progress through the streets, scattering handfuls of gold among the throng which pressed around him.

So he came to the palace, where the Sultan was so impressed and agreeably surprised by his first sight of his new and unknown son-in-law that he descended three steps of his throne to prevent Aladdin from throwing himself at his feet, and embraced him with the most evident marks of his affection.

After some polite speeches had passed between them, the Sultan conducted Aladdin to a magnificent room, where a great feast had been prepared. The Sultan and Aladdin sat together, waited upon by the Grand Vizier and the nobles of the court. After this, the Sultan ordered the chief judge to attend and commanded him to draw up a contract of marriage between the Princess Badroulboudour and Aladdin.

When the judge had drawn up the contract with all the requisite forms, the Sultan asked Aladdin if he wished to remain in the palace and to conclude the ceremonies that day.

"O, mighty monarch," he replied. "I request you to permit me to defer my happiness until I have built a palace for the Princess that will be worthy of her merit and dignity. And I entreat your Majesty to have the goodness to point out a suitable location. I will then do everything necessary to get it finished with all possible haste and diligence.

"My son," answered the Sultan, "there is a large open space in front of my palace which I shall be delighted to let you have for the purpose." With these kind words, he again embraced Aladdin.

The young man then took leave of the Sultan and returned home in the same way as he had come, receiving acclamations from the people, who wished him all happiness and prosperity. Retiring to his room, he instantly rubbed the lamp and summoned the genie.

"Oh, genie," said Aladdin. "I have hitherto had every reason to praise the precision and promptitude with which thou hast executed whatever I have required. I now command thee to build me a palace as quickly as possible, opposite to that belonging to the Sultan and at a short distance from it; and let this palace be in every way worthy to receive the Princess Badroulboudour, my bride. I leave the choice of the materials and the design to thee. But on the top floor let there be a large chamber with four walls of gold and silver, and let there be six windows in each wall, twenty-three of which have their frames set with jewels of the first water. I wish this palace to have a large court in the front, another at the back, and a garden. Above all, be sure that there is a room well filled with money, both gold and silver. Stables I must also have, filled with the most beautiful horses; also grooms and attendants, and female slaves for the service of the Princess. Go, and return as soon as thy task is completed."

The sun had already gone down when Aladdin had finished giving his orders to the genie with regard to the construction of the palace. The very next morning, when day broke, Aladdin had scarcely risen before the genie presented himself.

"O, master," said he. "Your palace is finished. Come and see if it is to your liking."

The genie transported him there in an instant, and when Aladdin had examined the whole palace, which exceeded his utmost expectations, and had seen all the riches and magnificence it contained, he exclaimed: "O, genie, no one can be more satisfied than I am. There is only one thing which I did not mention before. It is, to have a carpet of the finest velvet laid from the gate of the Sultan's palace to the door of the apartment which is reserved for the Princess."

"I will return in an instant," replied the genie, and he had not been gone a moment before Aladdin saw the carpet he had ordered rolled out by invisible hands. The genie then carried Aladdin back to his own house.

The Sultan's porters, who came to open the gates and who were accustomed to see an open space where Aladdin's palace now stood, were much astonished at observing that space occupied by a new and magnificent building and at seeing a lovely velvet carpet, which seemed to stretch from its gateway to that of the Sultan's abode. The news of this wonder soon spread through the palace, and the Grand Vizier was no less astonished than were the rest. The first thing he did was to go to the Sultan, to whom he tried to represent the whole business as enchantment. The Sultan, however, replied: "After the display of riches we have seen, can you think it so extraordinary that my son-in-law should be able to build a palace in this short time? He wished, no doubt, to surprise us, and every day we see what miracles riches can perform."

When Aladdin had returned home and dismissed the genie, he found that his mother was up and had begun to put on one of the magnificent dresses he had ordered for her the day before, and in which she admired herself immensely. When her toilet was completed, she proceeded to the palace in order to wait upon her new daughter-in-law. Aladdin then mounted his horse and left his father's house, never more to return; but he did not forget to take with him his wonderful lamp, which had been the cause of all his happiness and prosperity.

Aladdin's mother was received with great ceremony, and was taken by the chief steward to the apartment of the Princess Badroulboudour, who ran and embraced her and made her sit on her own couch. The Sultan also treated her with great courtesy and respect, being much struck, after her former humble appearance, at finding her as magnificently dressed as the Princess, his daughter.

When evening approached, the Princess took leave of the Sultan, her father, and began her progress to her new dwelling, with Aladdin's mother on her left hand, followed by a hundred female slaves, all beautifully dressed, and accompanied by bands of music and four hundred pages carrying torches.

In this way did the Princess proceed, walking upon the carpet which extended from the Sultan's palace to that of Aladdin, until she arrived at her

The genie appeared the instant Aladdin
rubbed the lamp (page 137)

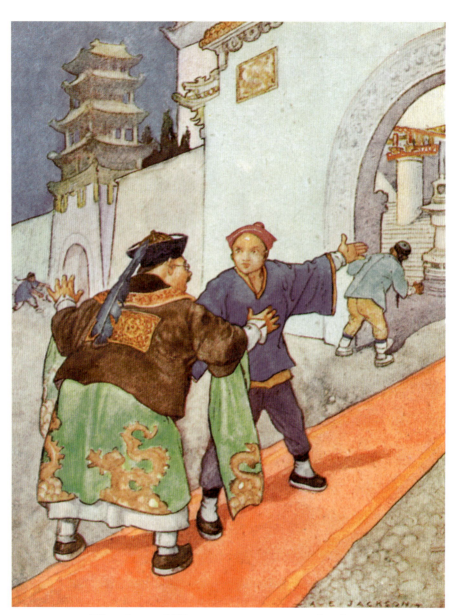

The Grand Vizier was as astonished as
everyone else (page 143)

destination, where Aladdin ran, with every expression of joy, to welcome her.

"O, adorable Princess," he cried. "If I should have had the misfortune to displease you by my boldness in aspiring to an alliance with the daughter of my Sultan, please consider that it was to your beautiful eyes and to your delightful charms alone that you must attribute my rashness.

"O, Prince, for thus I must now call you," replied the Princess. "I obey the will of the Sultan, my father, and now that I have seen you, I freely own that I obey him without reluctance."

Aladdin was delighted at this charming answer. He kissed the Princess's hand and then conducted her into a large chamber where there was a table spread with everything rare and delicious, and where all the dishes, cups and other articles were of solid gold.

The Princess Badroulboudour, Aladdin, and his mother sat down to table, where, as they feasted, they were entertained by a concert provided by invisible performers, arranged by the genie.

It was nearly midnight when, according to the custom at that time observed in China, Aladdin rose and presented his hand to the Princess Badroulboudour that they might dance together, and thus finish the ceremony of their wedding.

The next morning Aladdin went to his father-in-law's palace and begged him to do him the kindness of taking breakfast with him.

The Sultan readily granted this request, as he was anxious to see the inside of the palace Aladdin had built. He was much struck by the beauty of the exterior, but his expression of surprise and pleasure grew louder and higher as he passed from room to room. When he came to the chamber with the twenty-three casements of gems, he was so much astonished that he stood absolutely still.

"Nowhere," he exclaimed, "will anything be found to equal this. This palace is one of the wonders of the world. There is, however, one thing at which I am astonished, and that is, to observe that one of the windows is unfinished. Is it through forgetfulness, or neglect, or because the workmen have not had time to put the finishing strokes to this beautiful specimen of architecture?"

"My Lord," answered Aladdin, "it is left unfinished on purpose, as I wish your majesty to put the finishing stroke to the palace, that I may thus have a memento of the grace I have received from you."

"If you have left it with that view," replied the

Sultan, "I will give the necessary orders with the greatest of pleasure."

Aladdin then conducted him to the chamber where he had entertained the Princess Badroulboudour on the previous evening, and where two tables were set in the most magnificent manner. The Sultan sat at the first table and ate with his daughter, Aladdin, and the Grand Vizier, while the rest of the court officials were regaled at the second table.

Now, although Aladdin had requested the Sultan to complete the twenty-fourth window in the gold and silver chamber, he knew that he would be unable to make it match the others. And it was so; for, though the Sultan summoned the chief gem workers and goldsmiths in the kingdom, and furnished them with the finest of his jewels, they were only able to finish about half of it. Aladdin, therefore not only made them stop working, but also to undo all they had done and carry back the jewels to the Sultan.

Then he took out the lamp, rubbed it, and ordered the genie to complete the work. This the genie did in the twinkling of an eye, so that when the Sultan, who had been much surprised at the report of the craftsmen, and the return of the jewels, came to inquire into the matter, he was still more amazed to find the work done.

"My dear son," he cried in astonishment, "what a man you are, who can do such wonderful things almost immediately! There is not your equal in the world."

As time went on, Aladdin, by his kindness, courtesy and generosity, became beloved by all who came in contact with him. And so several happy years passed quickly by.

And now it is time to refer to one who, it may be thought has passed right out of the story, and that is the magician.

For some years he had remained in the belief that Aladdin had perished in the cavern in which he had imprisoned him. But about this time it occurred to him to make certain.

When, by means of his magic, he discovered that Aladdin was not only alive, but living in dignity and great wealth, he was greatly enraged, especially as he had no doubt that Aladdin owed all his good fortune to the lamp.

Therefore, the very next day, he started for China with the intention of revenging himself fully on Aladdin.

He arrived at the city where Aladdin lived and was soon in possession of most of the facts which have been related.

He visited and inspected the wonderful palace, and, filled with fury at this evidence of the fortune and greatness of Aladdin, he determined at all costs to obtain possession of the lamp which had wrought these wonders.

His first object was to discover its whereabouts. His magic art soon informed him that the lamp was in Aladdin's palace, and his joy was so great on learning this that he could hardly contain himself. "I shall get this lamp," he cried "and then I will fling the fellow back into the obscurity and poverty from which he has taken so high a leap.

It happened, most unfortunately for Aladdin, that just at this time he was absent on a hunting expedition which was to last several days.

As soon as the magician had discovered this, he went to the shop of a man who made and sold lamps.

"I want a dozen copper lamps," he said.

The man replied that he did not have that many in his shop, but if his customer would wait till the next day, he would have them ready for him, very well polished.

The next morning the magician collected the twelve lamps. He put them in a basket he had provided for the purpose, and went with this on his arm to the area of Aladdin's palace. Here he walked to and fro, crying with a loud voice: "Who will exchange old lamps for new ones?" All who passed laughed at his apparent folly. "That man," said they, "must surely have lost his senses to offer to exchange new lamps for old."

The magician was not surprised at the ridicule with which he was greeted. He seemed only intent on disposing of his merchandise, and continued to cry: "Who will exchange old lamps for new?" He repeated this so often as he walked to and fro on all sides of the palace, that at last the Princess Badroulboudour heard his voice and sent one of her slaves to find out the reason for the noise and bustle.

The slave soon returned, laughing heartily. "O, Princess," she said, "there is a fool outside with a basket on his arm full of beautiful new lamps which he will not sell, but offers to exchange for old ones."

Another of the female slaves immediately said: "There is an old lamp on a shelf in one of the chambers which seems to belong to no one. If the Princess will give me leave, I will see whether this fellow is really fool enough to give me a new lamp for an old one."

The Princess, who, unfortunately, was ignorant of the value of the lamp which Aladdin usually kept locked up, consented and sent the slave, who, beckoning to the magician, said: "Give me a new lamp for this old one I have here."

The magician at once guessed that this was the very lamp he was seeking. He eagerly took it, and bade the slave choose which of the new ones she would have. She selected the brightest and biggest and carried it to the Princess in triumph.

The magician now having no further use for his load of lamps, left his basket in a tiny alley and made haste to find a quiet spot outside the city. He then drew the lamp from his bosom and rubbed it. The genie instantly obeyed the summons. "What are thy commands?" cried the genie.

"I command you," replied the magician, "instantly to take the palace which you have erected in this city, and transport it and me to the country of Africa."

When, on rising the next morning the Sultan looked out of the window and saw only an open space where the palace of Aladdin had stood, he thought at first he was dreaming, and rubbed his eyes. "I cannot be mistaken," he said to himself. "It was in this very place that I beheld it. If it has fallen, the materials would lie strewn around; and if the earth had swallowed it, we should have heard and still see some signs of disturbance."

He sent in haste for the Grand Vizier. "Look out of

the window," said the Sultan on his arrival, "and tell me if you can see Aladdin's palace."

The Grand Vizier was as much amazed as the Sultan had been. When he was quite sure the palace of Aladdin had disappeared, he said: "Your majesty may remember that I declared from the beginning that this palace was the work of magic."

The Sultan, who could not deny this, was the more angry with Aladdin.

"Where is this impostor, this wretch?" he exclaimed, "that I may strike off his head. Go and order thirty of my horsemen to bring him before me in chains."

The horsemen set out and met Aladdin who was returning from the chase, about five or six leagues from the city.

"Prince Aladdin," said the officer in command, "it is with the greatest regret that I must inform you that we have been sent to arrest you. We entreat you not to be angry with us for doing our duty, as we must."

This declaration astonished Aladdin beyond measure. He felt himself innocent, and asked the officer if he knew of what crime he was accused, but the officer replied that neither he nor his men could give him any information.

Thereupon Aladdin dismounted and said: "I

submit. Execute whatever orders you have received."

When the guards entered the suburbs, all the people who saw Aladdin led in chains like a criminal felt sure he was going to lose his head. As he was generally beloved, some seized swords, others whatever arms they could find and those who had no weapons whatever took up stones, and tumultuously followed the guards.

Thus Aladdin was brought before the Sultan, who commanded the executioner, who was already present by his orders, to strike off his head.

But, at the crucial instant, the Grand Vizier called the Sultan's attention to the fact that a great crowd had overcome the guards and were preparing to storm the palace.

The Sultan was so alarmed at this that he ordered the executioner to sheath his sword, and take the bandage off Aladdin's eyes, and to set him free.

When Aladdin found himself free, he raised his hands in supplication and entreated the Sultan to tell him for what crime he had just pardoned him. "Thy crime, perfidious wretch!" exclaimed the Sultan. "Follow me, and I will show thee."

He led Aladdin to a window. "You know where your palace stood," he said. "Look around, and tell me what has become of it."

Aladdin looked, but saw nothing except the space which his palace had lately occupied.

"O, mighty king," replied Aladdin. "I see it has disappeared, but I can assure your majesty that I had no part whatever in taking it away."

"I care not what has become of your palace," replied the Sultan. "I esteem my daughter a million times beyond that, and unless you discover and bring her back to me, be assured your head will be chopped off."

"Great king," said Aladdin. "I entreat your majesty to grant me forty days to make the most diligent inquiries, and if I do not, within that period, succeed in my search, I will lay my head at the foot of your throne that you may dispose of me according to your pleasure."

"I grant your request," answered the Sultan, rather reluctantly.

Aladdin left the Sultan's presence in the deepest distress and humiliation.

For three days he roamed around the city, eating only what was given him in charity, and unable to come to any decision.

At length, as he could not bear to remain longer in a place where he had lived in such riches, he bent his steps toward the country. He came, toward the close of day, to the bank of a river. "Where shall I go to seek my palace?" he murmured to himself. "In what part of the world shall I find either my dwelling or my dear Princess?" The bank was steep and slippery, and as he spoke, he slipped. It was lucky for him that he still had on his finger the ring the magician had given him, for, in grasping a projecting stone to save himself, he rubbed the ring, and the same genie instantly appeared whom he had seen before in the underground cavern. "What are thy commands?" cried the genie.

Aladdin was most agreeably surprised by the sight of this unexpected help. He instantly replied: "Save my life, genie, a second time, by transporting me to the spot where my palace is and placing me under the window of the Princess Badroulboudour's room." As soon as he had said the words, the genie took him up and transported him to Africa, in the vicinity of a great city. In the midst of a large meadow in which the palace now stood, he set him down directly under the window of the Princess, and there left him.

As it was then night, Aladdin lay down under a tree to wait for daylight. Being now full of hope, he soon fell asleep.

The Princess Badroulboudour rose next morning much earlier than she had done since she had been transported to Africa by the artifice of the magician, whose hated presence she was compelled to endure once every day. When she was dressed, one of her women, looking through the lattice, perceived Aladdin, who was gazing up, and instantly ran to tell her mistress the glad news. The Princess, who could scarcely believe the fact, immediately went to the window and saw him herself. She opened the lattice, and Aladdin greeted her with the greatest joy. "Lose not a moment!" cried the Princess, "They have gone to open the secret door."

This secret door was directly below the rooms of the Princess. Aladdin entered, and in another instant all their troubles were forgotten in the joy of being together again.

At length, Aladdin said: "Before you speak of anything else, my Princess, tell me what has become of that old lamp which I left upon a shelf before I went hunting?"

"Alas! my dear husband," replied the Princess. "I greatly fear our misfortunes are connected with that lamp, and what distresses me more is that it was I who meddled with it."

She then gave Aladdin an account of all that had happened regarding the exchange of the old lamp for a new one. Then she told how, on the following night, she had felt the palace flying through the air, and had found herself next morning in Africa, a fact she had learned from the magician.

"O, Princess," replied Aladdin, interrupting her, as she was again blaming herself for all that had occurred. "The fault was mine for not having left the lamp hidden safely. But tell me, if you can, where he keeps it."

"He constantly carries it next to his chest," replied the Princess. "I am sure of this because he once took it out in my presence, showing it as a sort of trophy when he was trying to persuade me to be faithless to you, and to take him for my husband. But he never had any answer from me save disdain."

"My Princess," interrupted Aladdin. "I trust I have discovered the means of delivering you from our enemy. For this purpose, however, I must go into the town. Watch for my return."

Aladdin took the road that led to the town and when he got there, he went into a lane full of the shops of apothecaries. Entering the best shop, he asked the owner if he could sell him a certain powder.

The merchant replied that he kept it, but that it was very dear. Aladdin therefore took out his purse and purchased half an ounce for a piece of gold. Returning to the palace, where the secret door was opened instantly, he informed the Princess of the plan he had arranged for her deliverance.

"You must," he said, "attire yourself in one of your finest dresses, and when the magician pays you a visit, receive him with all the affability you can assume. Give him to understand that you are making the greatest efforts to forget me, and that he may be the more convinced of your sincerity, invite him to dine with you. But tell him that you have no wine fit for the occasion. On hearing this, he will leave you to procure some. In his absence, you must put this powder into one of the cups. Then, upon the first opportunity, you must fill it with wine and induce him to drink it. Scarcely will he have emptied the cup when you will see him fall backward."

The Princess promised to carry out these directions, and Aladdin took his leave.

As soon as he was gone, the Princess made her women dress her in the most becoming manner. She put on her richest attire, choosing those ornaments which set off her beauty to the greatest advantage; and when the magician made his appearance at his usual hour, she rose to greet him in all the glory of her beauty and her gorgeous array. She pointed to the best seat, and altogether treated him with a civility she had never before shown him.

When he had taken his seat, the Princess looked at him with an air of kindness, which made him suppose she no longer felt angry with him, and then said to him: "You are doubtless surprised at the change in me. But I have been thinking matters over and have decided that, as my father, in his rage, has doubtless put Aladdin to death, and as, therefore, an ocean of tears would be unavailing, I will shed no more, but make the best of things as they are. I, accordingly, begin by inviting you to supper. But, as I have no wine worthy of the occasion, I must ask you to supply that yourself."

The magician, who had never flattered himself that he would so soon and so easily acquire the good graces of the Princess, hastened to accept the invitation. "I will go and ferch two bottles and return immediately," he said.

"The longer you are gone, the more impatient I shall be to see you again," replied the Princess.

Delighted beyond measure, the magician hastened to bring the wine, while the Princess threw the powder which Aladdin had given her into a goblet, and set it aside until she had call for it.

On the magician's return, they sat down to supper, the Princess paying every attention to her guest.

Then, having given one of her women the signal to

fill the cup she had prepared with wine, she said: "In China, when two lovers drink together, they change goblets, and then drink to each other's health." With these words, she presented to her companion the goblet she held, and put out her other hand to receive his. The magician hastened to make the exchange and, having drained the cup to the last drop, fell back dead in his chair.

The Princess then ordered one of her women to admit Aladdin, who opened the robe of the magician, took out the lamp and rubbed it. The genie instantly presented himself and made his usual profession of service.

"O, genie," said Aladdin, "I command you, in the name of this lamp, to take this palace and transport it to the same spot in China from which it was brought."

The genie testified his obedience, and the journey was made immediately. Only two slight shocks were perceptible: one when the palace was taken up from the place where it stood in Africa, the other when it was set down in China, opposite the Sultan's palace. And this was all the work of little more than an instant.

Since the disappearance of Aladdin's palace and the loss of the Princess Badroulboudour, whom he

Aladdin was at the same table as
the Sultan (page 149)

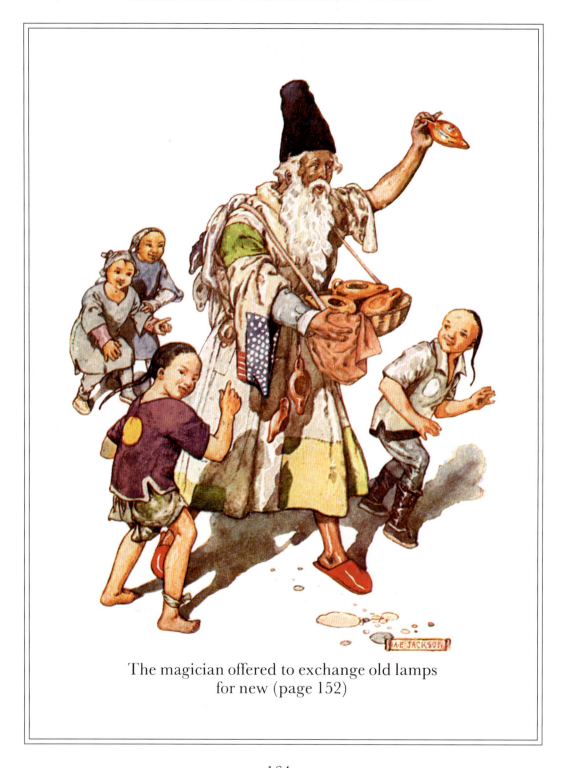

The magician offered to exchange old lamps
for new (page 152)

did not hope to see again, the Sultan had been inconsolable. Every morning, as soon as he had risen, he went to look out of the window in the direction where the palace of Aladdin had stood. When, on the morning following the events just described, he found the space no longer empty, he could not believe his eyes. But, when convinced that it was no delusion, his joy was so great that, without waiting for his attendants, he started off, and was received by Aladdin at the door of his palace.

"O, Aladdin," cried the Sultan. "I cannot speak to you till I have embraced my dear daughter."

The Princess had just finished dressing when the Sultan entered. He eagerly embraced her while the Princess, on her part, showed the greatest delight at again beholding him, and gave an exact account of all that had taken place from the moment the magician had been heard crying, "New lamps for old!" outside the palace.

At the conclusion of her story, the Sultan expressed his astonishment over and over again. Then, having again embraced Aladdin and his daughter, he returned to his palace and ordered a grand festival, to last for ten days, to celebrate the occasion.

In due course the Sultan died, and the Princess

came to the throne, sharing her power with Aladdin. They were beloved by everybody, and lived happily for very many years.

THE SLEEPER AWAKENED

uring the reign of the Caliph Haroun Alraschid, there lived in Baghdad a very rich merchant, whose wife was far advanced in years. They had an only son Abou Hassan. On his father's death, which occurred when he was thirty years of age, he came into the possession of great wealth, half of which he invested in land and houses, while the rest he decided to spend on enjoyment.

This he did so thoroughly that, in twelve months, all the money was spent. When he could no longer give feasts and entertainments, his friends forsook him.

In order to test them, he visited each and begged for a small loan. But none of those whom he had so lavishly entertained would assist him in his days of need. Some even pretended not to know him.

Abou Hassan therefore resolved, in future, to show no more hospitality to the people of Baghdad, but he determined that each day he would take a certain sum from the money he had kept in reserve, and offer supper and a night's lodging to some stranger.

This he did for some time. One day, a little before sunset, as he was seated in his usual manner on the bridge of Baghdad, he saw a serious, respectably dressed man approaching along the street, followed by a slave. This was none other than the Caliph Haroun Alraschid, who delighted to go around the city in disguise, looking for adventure.

Abou Hassan, taking him to be a merchant from the next town, saluted him and invited him to supper and to stay the night at his house. This invitation the Caliph cordially accepted.

So he took the disguised Caliph home and gave him a very good supper of roast goose, which had been cooked to a turn by Abou Hassan's mother. After this he brought out a bottle of good wine and, filling the Caliph's glass and his own, observed, "Any man who looks at you can tell that you are one of those who have seen the world and know how to enjoy it. I count the day fortunate on which I met you."

The Caliph, who was much amused by Abou Hassan, then asked him his name and what his employment was, and how he passed his time. Abou Hassan replied by giving a full account of himself and of the circumstances which had caused him to offer hospitality to a stranger, as he took the Caliph to be.

Very well satisfied with this explanation, the Caliph said to Abou Hassan: "I commend your conduct highly. You should be the happiest man in the world with the fresh company you enjoy every day. Before we part, for perhaps I shall be gone from your house before you are awake tomorrow, let me have the satisfaction of saying how I appreciate the civility, the good cheer, and the hospitality with which you have treated me. I am only anxious to know in what way I can best prove my gratitude for, though I am but a merchant, as you see, I am in a position, either alone, or with the help of my friends, to be of assistance to others."

To this Abou Hassan replied: "My good friend, I am perfectly contented with my lot, so that I have only to thank you, both for your kind offers and the pleasure you have conferred upon me by taking refreshment in my house. I will say, nevertheless, that there is just one thing I wish. The Imam of the mosque in this district is a meddlesome hypocrite. He and four of his friends, instead of attending to their proper duties, are always spreading scandal about me. If," he added, laughing heartily, "I might be Caliph for one day, I would order that one hundred strokes on the soles of the feet be given to each of the four old men, and four hundred to the Imam himself, to teach them to mind their own business."

"Your wish pleases me," said the Caliph, also laughing. "And I hope it may come true. I feel certain that the Caliph would readily trust his power in your hands for twenty-four hours if he only knew of the excellent use you would make of the opportunity. But is it not time to go to bed?"

"We will retire," answered Abou Hassan, "as soon as we have finished this wine. And the only thing I ask of you when you leave the house tomorrow morning, if I should not have risen, is to shut the door after you."

While Abou Hassan was speaking, the Caliph, who had thought of a scheme which promised to give him much amusement, managed to drop a little powder into the wine which Abou Hassan had just poured into his cup, and which he now swallowed in one gulp. Scarcely had Abou set the cup on the table, when the powder began to take effect and he fell soundly asleep. The slave, previously referred to, who had been awaiting his master's orders, was now summoned by the Caliph, who said:

"Take this man on your shoulders, and follow me.

But be careful to notice the position of this house, that you may bring him back hither when I tell you to."

The Caliph, followed by the slave bearing Abou Hassan on his shoulders, went out of the house but he did not close the door as Abou Hassan had requested him to do. When the Caliph arrived at the palace, he entered by a private door and ordered the slave to carry Abou Hassan to his own apartment, where the officers of the bedchamber were in waiting. "Undress this man," said he to them, "lay him down in my bed."

He then gave some other orders, after which he sent for the Grand Vizier, Giafar, and said: "Giafar, I sent for you to warn you not to seem astonished when, at the audience tomorrow morning, you will see on my throne the man who is now asleep on my bed. He will be dressed in my robes of state. Address him as you would me, and treat him exactly as if he were the Commander of the Faithful and see the others do the same."

The next morning the Caliph, having by his own orders been wakened early, went to a small closet adjoining the room where Abou Hassan slept, and where he could hear and see all that took place. The officers who were to be present came in at the same time, and took their accustomed places.

Then the officer who was nearest Abou Hassan's pillow applied to the sleeper's nose a small piece of sponge dipped in vinegar.

Abou Hassan sneezed and opened his eyes and, as far as the dim light permitted, he saw himself in a large and magnificent chamber, where he lay upon a bed covered with crimson and gold, with a number of officers and richly dressed slaves in attendance.

At the sight of all this lavishness, Abou Hassan was astonished and bewildered. He looked upon the whole as a delightful dream, which was the result of the wish he had expressed the night before, so he shut his eyes again that he might continue dreaming.

But a slave drew near. "O, Commander of the Faithful," said he respectfully, "it is time to rise."

Abou Hassan, much astonished at this address, said to himself, "I am not asleep, I am awake," and sat up in bed.

At this moment, Mesrour, the chief of the slaves, came in. He bowed down before Abou Hassan with his face to the ground and said:

"Commander of the Faithful, unless your majesty is indisposed, you will now be pleased to rise and give audience as usual."

At this address, Abou Hassan was convinced that

he was not asleep, and demanded of Mesrour, "Whom are you addressing? I know you not; you must certainly take me for some other person."

"O, my most esteemed Lord," answered Mesrour, "is not your majesty the Commander of the Faithful? Surely some disagreeable dream has disturbed your majesty's repose."

Abou Hassan burst into such a fit of laughter at this speech that he fell back on his pillow, to the great amusement of the real Caliph.

After he had laughed till he was out of breath, Abou Hassan sat up again in bed, and, speaking to a little slave, said, "Tell me, if you can, who I am."

"O, mighty sovereign," was the answer. "Your majesty is, indeed, the Commander of the Faithful, and Lord of all."

"Then bite my finger," said Abou Hassan, holding out his hand, "that I may know for certain whether I am asleep or awake."

The little slave trembled, but he obeyed, and bit sharply.

Abou Hassan drew back his hand in haste. "I am not asleep," he cried. "By what miracle have I become Caliph in one night?" Then, raising his voice, he demanded, "Tell me, all of you, am I truly the Caliph?"

And one and all replied, "Your majesty is in truth Commander of the Faithful."

"You are all untruthful," said Abou Hassan. "All the same, I will rise." The officers whose business it was to dress the Caliph speedily performed their office. Then, splendidly arrayed and preceded by Mesrour, he passed into the council chamber and ascended the throne.

As soon as Abou Hassan entered the council chamber, the Caliph left the closet in which he had been concealed and made his way to another one from which he could see and hear all that took place.

When Abou Hassan had taken his seat and the chief officers of the court had entered, the Grand Vizier prostrated himself at the foot of the throne, and said: "O, Commander of the Faithful, may Allah pour upon your majesty all the blessings of this life before receiving you into paradise."

After this address, Abou Hassan no longer doubted that his wish had been fulfilled, and that he was really the Caliph.

Then the Grand Vizier began to make his report of various matters. This report was a matter of routine, and of little consequence. Nevertheless, the real Caliph was in constant admiration of Abou Hassan's conduct, for he never appeared at all embarrassed, but gave just decisions upon the questions which came before him.

Before the Vizier had finished his report, Abou Hassan caught sight of the chief officer of the police.

"Stay a moment," said he, interrupting the Grand Vizier. "I have an order of importance to give. Let the chief officer of the police go to a certain street" (and he gave the name of his own street). "There, at the mosque, he will find the Imam and four old greybeards. Let the last four each have a hundred strokes on the feet, and let the Imam have four hundred. Then cause all five to be clothed in rags and mounted on a camel, with their faces turned toward the tail. Thus equipped, you shall have them led through the different quarters of the town preceded by a crier, who shall proclaim with a loud voice: "This is the punishment for those who meddle with affairs which do not concern them, and who make it their business to cause strife and mischief among people.""

The officer of police placed his hand upon his head to signify that he was ready to execute the order he had received, and departed.

The Grand Vizier went on with his report, which he had nearly ended, when the officer of the police returned and said: "O, Commander of the Faithful, everything has been done as you commanded."

Whereupon Abou Hassan said to the Grand Vizier: "Let the Grand Treasurer make up a purse of a thousand pieces of gold, go with it to the same quarter of the city, and give it to the mother of one Abou Hassan."

Then, the audience being over, he was conducted to a magnificent chamber where he was waited on by many very beautiful damsels, and where a band of female musicians played on a number of instruments in a most enchanting manner. Abou Hassan then feasted on the most delicious food he had ever had from golden dishes, and drank the rarest wines from a golden cup, all the time under the observation of the Caliph.

Then water was poured from a golden pitcher by one slave into a golden bowl held by another so that he might wash his hands, which he dried on a gold-fringed napkin held for him by a third slave.

The rich food and wine, of which he had partaken so freely, now began to make Abou Hassan drowsy. When one of the damsels saw his eyelids begin to droop, she went behind his back and dropped a little of the same powder which the Caliph had used the night before into a cup which she filled with wine, and offered it to him, saying: "Commander of the Faithful, I entreat your majesty to take this glass of wine, and also deign to listen to a song which I desire to sing to you."

"I grant both your requests with pleasure," said Abou Hassan, and drained the cup at one gulp. The damsel took her lute and sang a song of which Abou Hassan only heard the first new notes, being again suddenly overcome by sleep as profound as that he had experienced the night before.

The Caliph, who had derived more amusement from all this than he had expected, then came out of his hiding place. He first ordered that the Caliph's habit, in which Abou Hassan had been dressed in the morning, should be taken from him, and that he should be clothed again in the garments he had worn twenty-four hours before. He then ordered the slave to be called and said: "Take charge once more of this man, and carry him back to his own bed as silently as you can and without waking him up, and when you come away be careful to leave the door open."

Abou Hassan slept till very late the next day. Then, on opening his eyes, he was much surprised to find himself at his own house.

He raised his voice and called loudly and his mother came running in.

"What is the matter with you, my son?" she asked.

At these words Abou Hassan raised his head, and, looking at his mother with an air of haughtiness, replied "Good woman, who is the person you call your son?"

"You are he," answered she.

"I your son!" cried Abou Hassan. "You know not what you are saying. I am the Commander of the Faithful."

"Ah! cried the mother, "you utter words which clearly prove that you are not in your right mind. Do you not see that you are in your own room in the house in which you were born?

But Abou Hassan cried angrily: "I am not thy son, nor art thou my mother. I tell thee I am Commander of the Faithful, and thou shalt not make me believe otherwise nor contradict me."

"For heaven's sake, my son," she replied, "refrain from this kind of language lest some mischief befall you. Let us rather talk of something else. Allow me to tell you what happened yesterday to the Imam of our mosque, and to the four old men."

And she gave him a full account of the occurrence.

But the recital, far from effacing the notion that he was Commander of the Faithful, served only to impress it still more deeply.

"Know then," he declared, "that it was by my

orders that the Imam and the four old men were punished in the manner you have related. I tell you in good truth, I am the Commander of the Faithful, and all your reasoning will never persuade me to the contrary."

His mother, who felt quite sure that he had lost his senses, said: "My son, I pray heaven to pity and have mercy upon you. What would be said if you should be heard talking in this manner? You are my son, Abou Hassan, and you are wrong in claiming for yourself a title which belongs only to the Caliph Haroun Alraschid, especially as, only yesterday, the Grand Vizier himself brought me a purse of a thousand pieces of gold, bidding me to bless the Commander of the Faithful, who bade him make me this present."

At these last words Abou Hassan lost all command over himself.

"What!" cried he, "wilt thou not be convinced when I tell thee that I am the person who sent those thousand pieces of gold by my Grand Vizier, Giafar, who merely executed the order which I gave him as Commander of the Faithful? But I will not suffer thy insolence any longer."

Upon this he was so unnatural as to beat her, calling out at every stroke, "Am I the Commander of the Faithful? Answer me immediately with the truth."

And each time his mother replied, "You are my son."

Her cries brought the people from next door, who, on his still declaring that he was the Commander of the Faithful, were convinced that he was mad. So, having first bound him hand and foot, they sent for the keeper of the hospital for lunatics, who came at once with several assistants and, having handcuffed Abou Hassan, took him away with them.

Thus Abou Hassan was conveyed to the hospital where he was closely confined, and, as he still continued to assert that he was the Commander of the Faithful, he received fifty strokes of the whip each day.

Abou Hassan's mother came to see him every single day, and she could not refrain from crying to see his condition. She did her best to try to bring him to his senses, and at the end of about three weeks, he began to waver in his belief.

"If I were Caliph and Commander of the Faithful," said he to himself, "why would I have found myself, after my sleep, at my own house, and dressed in my own clothes? And yet I certainly ordered an officer of the police to punish the Imam and the four old men; and I ordered the Grand Vizier, Giafar, to

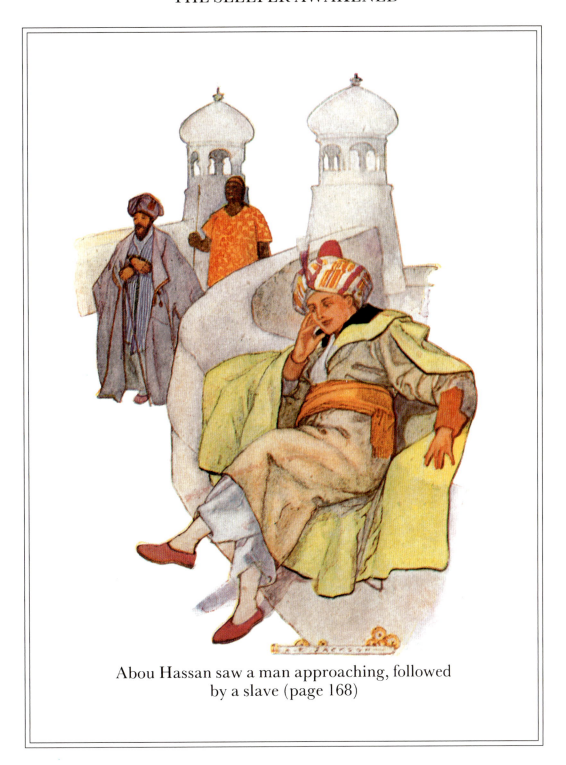

Abou Hassan saw a man approaching, followed
by a slave (page 168)

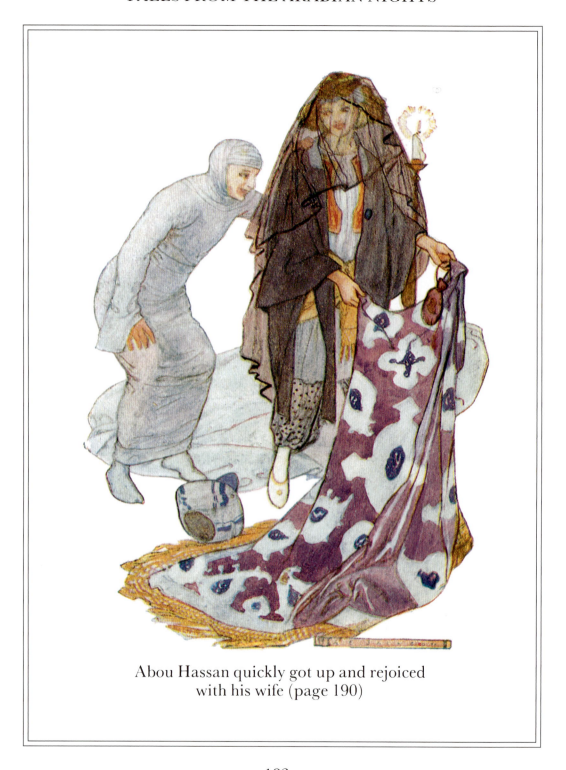

Abou Hassan quickly got up and rejoiced
with his wife (page 190)

carry a thousand pieces of gold to my mother, and my orders were obeyed. I cannot understand it in the least."

One day Abou Hassan was absorbed in these thoughts and reflections when his mother came to see him.

"Well, my son," said she, "how do I find you today? Have you given up all those foolish fancies?"

"O, my dear mother," answered Abou Hassan, "I acknowledge my error, and I entreat you to forgive me. I have been deceived by a dream, and am now convinced that I am not Commander of the Faithful, but your own son, Abou Hassan. And, since I am now perfectly restored to my senses, I entreat you to deliver me, as soon as may be, out of this cursed place of torment."

Abou Hassan's mother, overjoyed at her son's recovery, went immediately to seek the keeper of the madhouse, who, when she had assured him that her son was perfectly restored to his reason, released him.

Thus did Abou Hassan return to his house. But as soon as he had recovered a little he began to think it tiresome to pass his evenings without company. And so, on the first day of the month, he went again, toward sunset, to the foot of the bridge of Baghdad, in order to stop the first stranger who should approach and invite him to give him the pleasure of coming to dine at his house. It happened that this was again the day on which the Caliph amused himself by going around his city in disguise.

Abou Hassan had not long taken his seat when, casting his eyes toward the other end of the bridge, he saw the Caliph coming toward him in his old disguise of a merchant, and attended by the same slave who had formerly accompanied him to Abou Hassan's house. Convinced that all the misery he had suffered arose in some way from the wish he had expressed, and that this apparent merchant must be a magician, Abou Hassan trembled at the sight of him.

"Allah preserve me!" said he to himself. "If I am not mistaken, this is the very sorcerer who laid his spell upon me."

He therefore turned his head so that the man he supposed to be a merchant would not see him as he passed.

But the Caliph, who wished for a renewal of the amusement he had derived from Abou Hassan, and had taken great care to be informed of all that he had said and done after he awoke and was carried back to his house, came up to him and said:

"Do not you know me? Do not you recollect the evening we passed together, a month ago this very day, at your house, when you did me the kindness to entertain me so hospitably? Since I have been so fortunate to meet you a second time, you must again extend to me the hospitality you then showed me."

Abou Hassan shook his head and said, "You have done me much harm, and I fear to expose myself to more at your hands."

"My good friend," returned the Caliph, "how can that be? I beseech you to be convinced of my friendship, and tell me all that has happened to you."

Abou Hassan then gave the Caliph a full account of his wonderful dream, as he called it, and its disagreeable consequences. When Abou Hassan had finished, the Caliph said: "My dear friend, in spite of this, I wish again to have the pleasure of being your guest. Tomorrow, if it please heaven, all will be found to have turned out for the best."

"I consent," said Abou Hassan, "on two conditions: one that you shut the door on leaving so that no evil spirit may enter and turn my brain, and the other that you will not express any more good wishes for me."

"I agree," said the Caliph.

Thus the Caliph and Abou Hassan again supped

together. And, as before, the Caliph drugged his host, who instantly fell into a deep sleep in which he was again conveyed to the palace and placed in the Caliph's bed.

Next morning, Abou Hassan was awakened by the sound of sweet music provided by a large company of musicians and singers and on opening his eyes, he found himself, to his unspeakable astonishment, back in the magnificent chamber where he had once been awakened to his consequent disadvantage.

"Allah preserve me!" he exclaimed. "I am once more bewitched. Perhaps, if I keep my eyes closed tightly, I shall escape further evil."

But two of the officers of the bedchamber took him respectfully but firmly by the arm, and, lifting him from his couch, placed him on a throne-like seat in the middle of the sumptuous chamber, as before.

Then all the instruments began to play at the same time, and the damsels and the officers began to dance and sing so that Abou Hassan became infected with the general excitement. Stripping off the fine robes of the Caliph in which they had arrayed him, he sprang off his couch, and taking two of the damsels by the hand, began to skip and dance with them so actively, and with so many droll and extravagant turns and twists that the Caliph, in his hiding place, laughed so violently that he fell backward, and his laughter was heard above all the noise of the musical instruments. Then, opening a lattice in his closet, the Caliph said still laughing: "Abou Hassan, Abou Hassan, are you determined to make me die with laughter?"

When the Caliph spoke everyone was silent, and the music ceased. Abou Hassan turned his head and, seeing the Caliph knew that it was he whom, disguised as a merchant, he had entertained the night before.

With ready wit, he fell in with the fun and design of the Caliph.

"Ah, ha!" cried he, "you are there then, my friend the merchant? But why do you complain? Surely it is better to die of laughter than to receive fifty strokes daily for three weeks, as I did."

"You are right," said the Caliph, coming forward. "And, by way of compensation, ask of me what you will."

"O, Commander of the Faithful," returned Abou Hassan, "the thing I ask is that you allow me free access to your person, that I may have the happiness of admiring your greatness all my life long."

This reply pleased the Caliph vastly. "I grant your request," he said. "You shall have an apartment in the palace and free access to me at all times."

As time went on, Abou Hassan grew closer and closer to the Caliph, who even sometimes brought him to visit his wife, Zobeidè. She had heard the whole story of the trick, which had entertained her much. Princess Zobeidè was very well pleased with Abou Hassan, and she observed that, whenever he attended the Caliph in his visits to her, he always had his eye on one of her damsels, whose name was Attar-of-Roses.

She communicated this to the Caliph, and, as Attar-of-Roses seemed equally attracted to Abou Hassan, a match was arranged between them and the marriage was celebrated at the palace with a great show.

Abou Hassan and Attar-of-Roses lived together very happily; but, both being of extravagant habits and denying themselves nothing, they found themselves very short of money at the end of a year having spent all of the generous amount which the Caliph had bestowed upon them at their marriage.

The Caliph's generosity had been so great that Abou Hassan was ashamed to ask him for more, o he informed his wife that he had thought of a plan which would amuse the Caliph vastly and, at the same time be profitable to themselves.

"I propose," he said, "that both of us should die."

"That both of us should die!" repeated Attar-of-Roses. "You may die, if you so please, but, for my part, I am not yet tired of life and choose to live for many more years."

"You give me no time to explain myself," replied Abou Hassan. "You must understand that I do not mean a real death, but only a pretend one. In order to carry out my scheme I am going to play the dead man. You must put me in a coffin as if I were actually dead, with my feet properly turned toward Mecca. When this has been done, you are to begin weeping and lamenting, rending your garments and tearing your hair, and in this state you shall present yourself to the Princess Zobeidè, who will pity you and give you enough money to provide for my funeral expenses. As soon as you have returned with this money, you shall take my place. You shall pretend to be dead, and, after you have been put into a coffin, I will go in my turn to the Caliph, and tell him the same tale you told the Princess."

"Let us lose no time," said Attar-of-Roses, clapping her hands. "While I am getting a shroud for myself, you take off your upper garments."

Abou Hassan lay down and was wrapped in the sheet in the manner which made him look as if he were only waiting to be carried out for burial. His wife turned his feet toward Mecca, covered his face with the finest muslin, then placed his turban over it in such a manner as not to interfere with his breathing. She then shrieked and lamented so loudly that the Princess Zobeidè heard her from her apartment, and sent to enquire whence the cries and lamentations proceeded. On being informed of the cause of her dearest damsel's grief, she sent for her with the intention of offering consolation, and ended by shedding tears herself.

"It is indeed sad," said the Princess, "that a man who appeared in such good health, and was so agreeable and amusing, should be dead so suddenly."

She then ordered that a purse of a hundred pieces of gold should be given to Attar-of-Roses, together with a piece of gold brocade long enough for a pall.

As soon as Attar-of-Roses was out of the presence of the Princess, she joyfully dried her tears and returned to give Abou Hassan an account of the success she had met with in playing her part. Abou Hassan quickly got up and rejoiced with his wife when he saw the purse and the piece of brocade. "I will now die in my turn," said Attar-of-Roses, very pleased with the result of her stratagem.

So Abou Hassan rose and laid out his wife in the

same manner as he himself had been, turned her feet toward Mecca, and went out of his chamber in great disorder, with his turban awry, like a man in great affliction. Thus he went to the Caliph with one hand holding a handkerchief to his eyes, and with the other violently beating his breast, while he uttered exclamations expressive of the greatest sorrow.

The Caliph, who was accustomed to see Abou Hassan with a cheerful countenance, at once asked the occasion of his grief.

On being informed, he showed considerable emotion, and wept with the bereaved husband, after which he ordered that a purse of a hundred pieces of gold and a piece of brocade should be given to him.

The Caliph then said to Mesrour, chief of the servants of the palace, "Come with me, and share in the grief of the Princess for the death of her slave Attar-of-Roses."

They went together to Princess Zobeidè's apartment and found her in tears.

The Caliph tried to console her, saying: "I know Attar-of-Roses had many good qualities which endeared her to you. But your sorrow cannot bring her back to life."

"Commander of the Faithful," the Princess replied in much surprise, "you are mistaken. Attar-of-Roses is in perfect health. My tears are for Abou Hassan, her husband, your pet, and the indifference I see you manifest at his death, and the forgetfulness you show in so little time, fill me with astonishment."

The Caliph began to laugh and said: "Shed no more tears for Abou Hassan, for he is perfectly well. It has scarcely been a moment ago since he came to me in tears to announce the death of his dear wife. I ordered a purse of a hundred pieces of gold and a piece of brocade to be given to him. Mesrour here was witness of all that happened."

"Commander of the Faithful," replied the Princess, "although it be your custom to jest, I must say that this is not a proper time to do so. It is not *my* slave who is dead, but her husband, Abou Hassan."

"And I," answered the Caliph, "tell you without jesting that it is Attar-of-Roses who is dead, and that Abou Hassan is alive and in perfect health."

"You are altogether wrong," she replied, with irritation. "It is not an hour since the wife of Abou Hassan left me. She came hither in despair, and I made her a present of a purse of a hundred pieces of gold and a piece of brocade."

The Caliph's eyes sparkled with anger. "Go," he said to Mesrour, "and see which of the two is dead, and instantly bring me word."

When Abou Hassan, looking through a lattice, saw Mesrour approaching, he told his wife to pretend to be dead once more, and to make her preparations quickly.

He had only just spread over her the piece of brocade which the Caliph had bestowed on him, when Mesrour entered the chamber.

The latter lifted the cloth which covered the body so that he might look at the face, and said: "Princess Zobeidè persisted in maintaining to the Caliph that it was you who were dead, and not your wife; and the Caliph sent me to try to ascertain the truth. I can assure you, I share very sincerely with you in your time of sadness."

As soon as the Caliph saw Mesrour, he demanded, "Tell us who is dead, the husband or the wife?"

"Commander of the Faithful," answered Mesrour, "it is Attar-of-Roses who is dead, and Abou Hassan is overwhelmed with grief."

But the Princess called her women. "Speak," she demanded, "and tell the Caliph who it was who came to me a short time before he made his visit here?"

The women all answered that it was the poor bereaved Attar-of-Roses.

Then she turned to the Caliph and said: "As I believe that you are in league with Mesrour, I beg you to allow me to send someone I can trust to Abou Hassan's apartments, that I may know whether I am really in error."

The Caliph gave his consent, and his wife sent her nurse on this important errand.

Meanwhile Abou Hassan, who had been keeping watch perceived the nurse at some distance. He called his wife and said: "Here comes your lady's nurse to enquire the truth. I must once more play the dead man."

The nurse, on entering, saw Attar-of-Roses in tears. Silently approaching, she raised the brocade, uncovered the face of Abou Hassan, and, after a few words of sympathy, departed. Scarcely had she closed the door when Attar-of-Roses had wiped her eyes, and took off the things in which Abou Hassan was wrapped, after which they both sat down to wait for what would happen next.

Princess Zobeidè heard the nurse's report with a satisfaction she could not conceal, while the Caliph was much puzzled.

Finally he said, "Let us go ourselves, that we may see with our own eyes on which side the truth lies."

The Princess followed him and Mesrour walked in front of them to open the door. Abou Hassan saw them coming, and immediately warned his wife of this so they could plan what they should do next.

"Let us now," he said, "both pretend to be dead, and you shall see that all will turn out well."

So Abou Hassan and his wife placed themselves one beside the other, in the middle of the chamber, each under a piece of brocade, and waited quietly for the arrival of the company.

The illustrious visitors presently appeared. Mesrour opened the door and the Caliph and Princess Zobeidè entered the chamber, followed by their attendants. They were much surprised, and stood silent for a time, looking at the dismal spectacle presented to their view.

Princess Zobeidè at last broke silence. "Alas!" said she to the Caliph, "both are dead. My poor Attar-of-Roses has died of grief at the loss of her husband."

"Say, rather," reply the Caliph, "that she died first, and that Abou Hassan expired of affliction."

"Nothing of the kind," persisted the Princess. "You are altogether wrong."

This obstinacy so provoked the Caliph that he exclaimed, "I swear that I will give a thousand pieces of gold to the person who shall ascertain for me which of the two died first."

The Caliph had scarcely said these words when he heard a voice cry, "Commander of the Faithful, it was I who died first. Give me the thousand pieces of gold."

At the same time, Abou Hassan freed himself from his covering and threw himself at the Caliph's feet. His wife rose in the same manner, and ran to throw herself at the feet of Zobeidè, who gave a cry of alarm. The Caliph, on the contrary, became speechless with laughter, and when he found utterance exclaimed, "Abou Hassan, Abou Hassan, have you determined to make me die with laughter? How came it into your head to play us such a trick?"

"Commander of the Faithful," replied Abou Hassan, "I will tell you the whole truth without disguise."

He did so; and the Caliph who, far from being angry, had not ceased laughing, said: "I will willingly give you the thousand pieces of gold I promised, for the joy I feel that neither of you is dead."

"And I," said the Princess Zobeidè, "will also give a thousand pieces to my dear Attar-of-Roses as a token of my own joy."

After that, the Caliph and the Princess took care that their pets had ample supplies of gold to meet all their reasonable requirements, and Abou Hassan and his wife lived even more happily than before.

THE ENCHANTED
HORSE

O nce upon a time there was a King of Persia named Sabur, who had one son and one daughter. The son, whose name was Feroze-shah, and who was the apple of his father's eye, was not only the handsomest, but also the bravest and most amiable Prince in all the world.

On the first day of the year, which was observed as a festival, the King was in the habit of holding a public audience at which he received gifts and congratulations, and bestowed pardons and rewards.

On one of these occasions, a Hindu from a distant land presented himself before the King with a horse made of ebony, inlaid with ivory. This horse was so well carved that it almost seemed to be alive.

The King was delighted with its appearance, and at once offered to buy it.

But the Hindu, prostrating himself before the King, explained that this was an Enchanted Horse, which would carry the rider wherever he wished to go in the shortest possible time. He added that he was willing to part with it on one condition only; but, before stating that condition, he would give an exhibition of the creature's powers.

"Then mount," said the King, "and bring me a branch of the palm tree which grows at the foot of yonder hill." And he pointed to a hill about three leagues away.

The Hindu at once mounted, and, turning a small peg on the right side of the horse's neck, was instantly borne upward and carried through the air at a great height and with the speed of lightning, to the amazement of all the beholders below.

In less than a quarter of an hour he was back with the palm branch, which, on dismounting, he laid at the feet of the King, whose desire to possess this magic steed was now increased a hundred times, and who offered to pay whatever sum the other demanded.

"Sire," replied the Hindu, "There is only one thing I will take in exchange for this horse, which, as your Majesty perceives, is one of the wonders of the world."

"What is that?" inquired the King. "Name it, and it is yours."

"The hand of the Princess, your daughter," was the reply, which excited the ridicule of all who heard,

The Prince mounted, turned the peg, and rose
into the air (page 203)

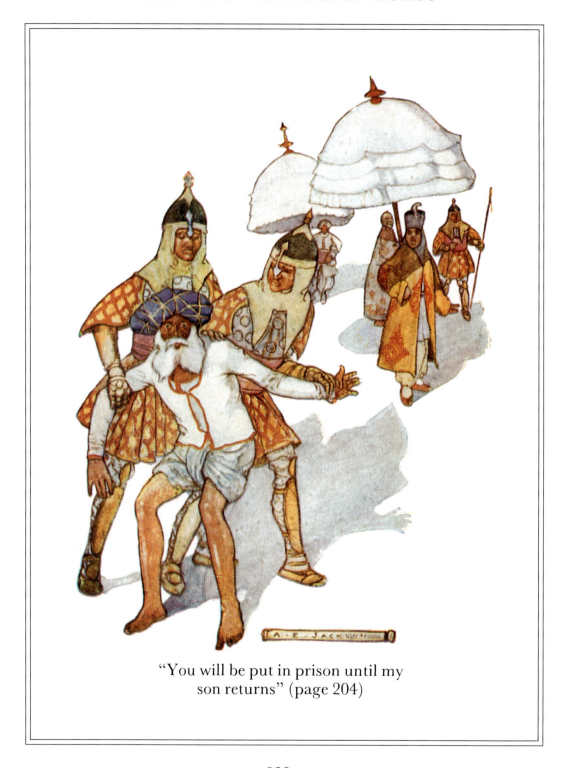

"You will be put in prison until my
son returns" (page 204)

The Prince left the Enchanted Horse
on the terrace (page 205)

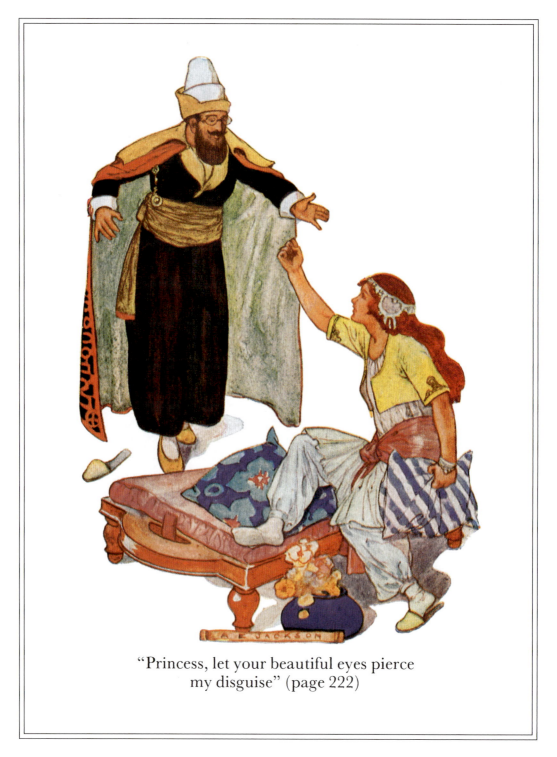

"Princess, let your beautiful eyes pierce
my disguise" (page 222)

for the Hindu was not only unpleasant in appearance, but also at least twice the age of the King, and the Princess, who was only fifteen, was as beautiful as she was charming.

Prince Feroze-shah, who stood beside the King, his father, was extremely indignant at this shocking request.

"I hope, my father," he said, "that you will not hesitate to refuse such an insolent demand, and will also chastise the maker of it."

"My son," replied the King, who had a craving for anything that was rare and curious, "I have no intention of granting the request. But, possibly, he is not really serious in making it, and would, instead accept the weight of the horse in gold. In any case, suppose you mount the horse yourself, so that you can give me your opinion of it."

The Prince was but too willing to agree, and the Hindu ran to assist him. But the Prince mounted without his assistance, and as soon as he had his feet in the stirrups, without waiting for any instructions, he turned the peg as he had seen the other do. Instantly the horse rose in the air as swift as an arrow, and in a few moments both horse and rider were out of sight.

The Hindu, alarmed at what had happened,

prostrated himself before the King, who was at once angry and alarmed at the disappearance of his son.

"Your majesty must admit that I was blameless," he said. "The Prince gave me no time to utter a word, or to point out to him a second peg by which the horse is guided and made to descend. It can also be guided by means of the bridle. But it is possible that the Prince may discover this for himself."

"Your own life shall answer for that of my son," said the King. "And until he returns or I hear some tidings of him, you will be put in prison, and fed on bread and water."

Meanwhile, the Prince was being carried so rapidly through the air that in less than an hour he was out of sight of the earth. He then thought it was time to return; so he pulled the bridle, and turned the peg with which he had started the horse the opposite way. When he found that this had no effect, but that the horse continued to ascend, he became alarmed.

He continued to turn the peg one way and another, but without arresting the horse's ascent, and it seemed as though, in time, he must be burned up by the sun. Then, to his great joy and relief, he discovered another, smaller peg behind the horse's other ear, and, turning this, his upward flight was instantly checked and he began to descend, but at a much slower rate, much to his great relief.

The sun was already setting, and it grew dark rapidly as he drew near the earth so that he was unable to see what was beneath him, whether a city, a desert, a plain, or a mountain top. It was equally possible that the horse might plunge with him into a lake, or river, or even into the sea. Consequently, when at the dead of night, the horse at last came to a stop and the Prince felt solid ground beneath his feet, he was inexpressibly relieved. He was also most agreeably surprised to find himself on the terrace of a magnificent palace, gleaming with white marble.

He was faint and hungry, having eaten nothing since the early morning, and at first could scarcely stand. But, leaving the horse, he groped his way along until he came to a staircase, which he found led downward, and at the foot of which was a half-open door through which a ray of light shone.

Descending as noiselessly as possible, the Prince paused at the door and, listening, heard the loud breathing of sleepers within. He advanced cautiously, and by the light of a lamp saw that the sleepers were black slaves. Their naked swords lay beside them, which was enough to show him that this was the guard chamber of some royal personage.

Proceeding on tiptoe, the Prince crossed the

chamber to a curtained archway, without waking any of the sleepers. Raising the curtain, he saw a magnificent chamber with a raised couch in the middle, while round the sides of the chamber were ranged low couches on which a number of female slaves were sleeping. The Prince crept softly toward the middle couch, and saw the most beautiful Princess in the world sleeping on her silken pillows, with her hair spread round her like a veil.

Falling on his knees, he remained entranced by her loveliness until the power of his gaze penetrated her closed eyelids, and, opening her eyes, she saw the handsomest Prince in the world regarding her in an ecstasy of admiration.

She showed the greatest surprise, but not the least sign of fear. Observing this, the Prince ventured to address her in the most respectful manner.

"Beautiful Princess," he said, "you see at your feet the Prince of Persia, brought here by what he now regards as a most happy and fortunate adventure, and who implores your aid and protection."

"Prince," she replied, "the kingdom of Bengal, in which you now are, will afford you all the hospitality and assistance you may require. My father, the Rajah, built this palace not far from his capital for the sake of the country air. Of this place I am absolute mistress, and I bid you welcome. At the same time, though I much desire to know by what means you have arrived here from such a far country as Persia, and by what magic you have evaded the vigilance of my guards, I am convinced that you must be in need of rest and refreshment. I will, therefore, direct my attendants to show you a quiet apartment where you may obtain both before you answer any of the many questions which I am dying to put."

Her attendants, though naturally much surprised at the sight of the Prince in their midst, at once carried out her commands, and he was conducted to a handsome room, where, after he had been supplied with the refreshment of which he was so much in need, he slept soundly until morning.

The Princess took great pains with her appearance next day, and altered her mind so often as to what she would wear, and, generally, gave so much trouble to her women that they plainly perceived what a strong impression the stranger must have produced.

When her mirror assured her that never had she appeared so charming, she sent for the Prince, and expressed a desire to hear what strange adventure had caused his appearance the night before.

The Prince was only too pleased to relate the story of the Enchanted Horse and all that had befallen him since he had mounted it. He concluded by thanking her for the kind and hospitable manner in which she had received him, and declared that it would now be his reluctant duty to return without delay and relieve the anxiety of his father.

The Princess would not agree to this, but urged him to stay a short time longer as her guest in order to see a little of the kingdom of Bengal, where he had so unexpectedly arrived, and of which he would then be able to give an account on his return to Persia.

The Prince could hardly refuse such a request from such a charming Princess, and so put off his return from day to day and from week to week, while the Princess entertained him with feasts, concerts, hunting parties, and every other form of amusement she could think of. In this way, the time flew so fast that the Prince was surprised and ashamed when one day he found that two months had passed, during which time his father must either have suffered the greatest possible anxiety, or else have concluded that his son was dead. Not another day would he consent to remain at the Palace and yet, he asked, how could he tear himself away from his "adorable Princess".

The Princess made no reply to this, beyond casting

down her eyes and blushing. Emboldened, the Prince then went on to ask whether he might dare to hope that she would return to Persia with him.

Without uttering a word, she gave the Prince to understand that she had not the least objection to this arrangement, though she afterwards admitted a little nervousness in case the Enchanted Horse might refuse to carry a double burden. But the Prince easily reassured her. He also declared that, with the experience he had gained on his journey, he was now quite capable of managing and guiding the horse as he desired.

The Princess thereupon consented to fly with him, and she arranged matters so that no one would have the slightest suspicion of their intentions.

Consequently, very early the next day, when all the other inhabitants of the palace were still sleeping, she stole from her room to the terrace, where both the horse and the Prince awaited her.

The Prince turned the horse toward Persia and, having first mounted himself, assisted the Princess to mount behind him. Then, when she was safely settled, with both her arms round his waist, he turned the peg, and the horse mounted into the air.

It flew as rapidly with two riders as with one, and in little more than two hours Prince Feroze-shah could distinguish the domes and minarets of the city of Shiraz, from which he had flown on the first day of the New Year.

He thought it better not to fly directly to the palace, and so alighted at a sort of pavilion, or summer palace, just outside the walls. Here he left the Princess while he went to break the happy news of his return to his father. Leaving the Enchanted Horse behind, he obtained another horse on which he rode; and, being recognized as he passed through the streets, was welcomed with shouts of joy by the people.

The news of his return preceded him, and he was received by the King, his father, with tears of joy. In as few words as possible, the Prince gave an account of all that had befallen him, including his sensations during the flight, his arrival at the palace of the Princess, and all the kindness and hospitality which had been shown to him since.

"If," replied the King, "there were any way by which I could show my gratitude to this lady, I would do it even if it cost me the half of my kingdom."

"My father," replied Prince Feroze-shah, "you have only to consent to my marriage to this charming Princess in order to assure the happiness of both. Indeed, I felt so sure of your consent that I induced her to accompany me on my return flight; and she is even now waiting for me at the summer palace. Allow me now to return and assure her that you will gladly welcome her as a daughter."

"Son," replied the King, "I not only consent most heartily, but will myself accompany you thither and escort her with due ceremony to my palace, where the marriage shall be celebrated this very day."

He then ordered that the Hindu should be brought from the prison, where he had been closely confined for the last two months, and set before him.

When this had been done, he said: "I swore that your life should answer for that of my son. Thanks be to God, he has now returned in safety. Go, take your Enchanted Horse, and never let me see your face again."

The Hindu had already learned, from those who had been sent to release him, of the return of the Prince from a far country, accompanied by a Princess, reported to be of great beauty. He was also able to make himself acquainted with the location of the summer palace, where she was now awaiting the Prince. The King had ordered him to take his horse and depart; and he now saw a means by which to obey the King, and, at the same time, revenge himself upon the monarch, as well as upon the Prince, to whom he also owed a grudge.

Consequently, while a procession, with instruments of music to accompany it, was being arranged and a magnificent litter prepared for the Princess, and while the King was putting on his grandest robes, and a feast being hastily set out, the Hindu, without losing an instant, started off for the summer palace, reaching it before the procession had begun to move on its slow and ceremonious way.

He soon discovered the whereabouts of the Princess, and, gaining an audience with her, announced that he had been sent by the Prince of Persia in order to bring her on the Enchanted Horse into the presence of the King, who with the whole of his court and all the inhabitants of the city, had assembled in the great square of the palace to view the marvel of her flight through the air.

The Princess did not hesitate a moment, thinking he had come from the Prince. She mounted at once; and the Hindu, placing himself before her, with many protestations of respect, turned the peg, and the horse soared upward.

At this moment, the King, the Prince and the entire court were about half-way to the summer palace, when, hearing a mocking laugh which seemed to come from overhead, the Prince glanced up. To his great surprise and distress, he saw the Enchanted Horse bearing the Princess and the Hindu high above the heads of the procession, which, on hearing the Prince's cry of anguish, came to a dead stop.

The King also saw the Hindu, and, furious at this insult to his dignity, hurled imprecations upon him as horse and riders rapidly dwindled to a speck in the clear blue sky.

The courtiers and other members of the procession added their voices, and produced such a tumult that it was heard all over the city, but the grief of Prince Feroze-shah was beyond words.

He returned to the palace, where for a time he shut himself up and refused to see anyone or to take any food. Then, seeing the uselessness of this action, he obtained the robe of a dervish through a trustworthy agent. For he had formed a plan to disguise himself and set out and search for his beloved Princess until he had found her, or had perished in the attempt. He knew not which way to go, but trusted Providence to direct him. So, furnishing himself with sufficient money and jewels to last a considerable period, he left his father's palace without informing anyone of his plan to find his Princess.

Meanwhile, the Princess, as soon as she found that, instead of being conducted to her Prince, she was being torn from him, had wept and implored her captor to restore her to her dear Feroze-shah. It was impossible to escape except by throwing herself from the horse's back, which she was loath to do. Thus, after a flight which lasted through the night, she found herself early next morning in the kingdom of Kashmir. The Hindu had descended in a wood outside the walls of the capital city, and the Princess now had a chance of getting help. So, in spite of all efforts to prevent her, she cried as loudly as she could, in the hope that someone would hear her and come to her assistance.

It happened, very fortunately, that the Sultan of that country, in returning from a hunting expedition, passed within earshot of her cries and went to her rescue.

He saw the Hindu struggling with the Princess, whom, in trying to stifle her voice, had half suffocated her, and demanded who he was, and why he was ill-treating the lady.

The Hindu, ignorant of the rank of the inquirer, replied insolently: "She is my wife, and I shall treat her as I please. It is no one's business to interfere."

But the Princess cried: "Do not believe him. I am a

Princess of Bengal, and was about to be married to the Prince of Persia when this wicked person, whom I believe to be a magician, carried me off by fraud by means of the horse you see yonder, which is enchanted. Whoever you are, have compassion on me and save me from this wicked man."

She had no need to urge the Sultan further. Her beauty, dignity and evident distress were all to her credit. Convinced of the truth of her appeal, and enraged by the insolence of the Hindu, the Sultan made a sign to his guards, who at once surrounded the now terrified Hindu, and put an end to his prayers for mercy by cutting off his head.

The Sultan then conducted the Princess to his palace, where she was sumptuously lodged, and received all the respect due to her beauty and high rank.

The Princess was overjoyed at her escape, and hoped the Sultan would at once take steps to restore her to the Prince of Persia.

But she was bitterly disappointed, for the Sultan, charmed by her appearance and manner, had resolved to marry her himself.

At break of day, she was awakened by the beating of drums, the blowing of trumpets, and other sounds of general rejoicing, which had been commanded for the occasion of the forthcoming royal wedding.

Later, when the Sultan came to inquire after the health of the Princess, she asked the meaning of all these festive sounds. When informed that they were part of the festivities for her marriage, she was struck speechless with dismay, and when the Sultan went on to ask her assent to what had already been arranged, she fainted away, which the Sultan took to be the effect of extreme joy.

When she came to herself, she resolved to feign madness in order to gain time. This she did by tearing her clothes and her hair, biting her cushions, and rolling on the floor. She even pretended to attack the Sultan with her fingernails, and alarmed him so much that he quitted her presence hurriedly and went to give orders to stop the drums beating and the blowing of the trumpets and to postpone all further preparations for the marriage.

Several times during the day he sent to inquire if the strange and violent attack which had so suddenly seized the Princess had passed off or lessened. But each time he was told there was no improvement, and that whatever change there might be was for the worse.

The next day, as the Princess still talked and acted very violently, the Sultan sent his own physicians, as well as those most famous in the city, to visit the patient and report on the case. But she not only refused to allow them to feel her pulse, or examine her tongue, but would not even let them approach her. So they came away looking very wise, but shaking their heads and declaring that the case was hopeless, and that if they could not cure her, nobody could. In spite of this, the Sultan sent far and wide for other physicians, who came, looked at the Princess (who became more violent at each visit), shook their heads, prescribed for her, and went away looking wiser than ever.

He even sent messengers to other kingdoms, offering munificent rewards and great promotion to anyone who could cure the Princess of her malady. But the result was always the same, and the Sultan began to despair, for all this only made him more and more anxious to marry the Princess.

Meanwhile, Prince Feroze-shah, disguised as a dervish, and plunged in grief, was wandering about the country, looking for his lost Princess. He roamed from province to province and from town to town, inquiring everywhere if anyone had seen or heard anything of an Enchanted Horse which could fly through the air, and describing its two riders. The result was that most of those he met and spoke to thought he was out of his mind, and, because he was handsome and amiable, pitied him.

At last, he was making his usual inquiries in a city of Hindustan, he heard the people talking of a certain Princess of Bengal who was to have been married to the Sultan of Kashmir had she not become violently mad on the wedding day.

At this, for to him it seemed that there could be only one Princess of Bengal, the Prince at once set out for the kingdom of Kashmir.

Arriving at the capital after many days, he took a humble lodging at an inn, where the talk again was all of the mysterious mad Princess with whom the Sultan was so much in love.

Mention was also made of the Hindu and his well observed fate, while the Enchanted Horse, it was reported, had been placed among the royal treasures. All these circumstances convinced the Prince of Persia that his lost Princess was found at last. The only difficulty was to be able to get to her. And even this was not a difficulty for long.

The number of physicians who had visited and prescribed in vain for their fair patient, great as it had been, was exaggerated by the gossips of the city. So it appeared to the Prince the easiest thing in the world to add himself to their number.

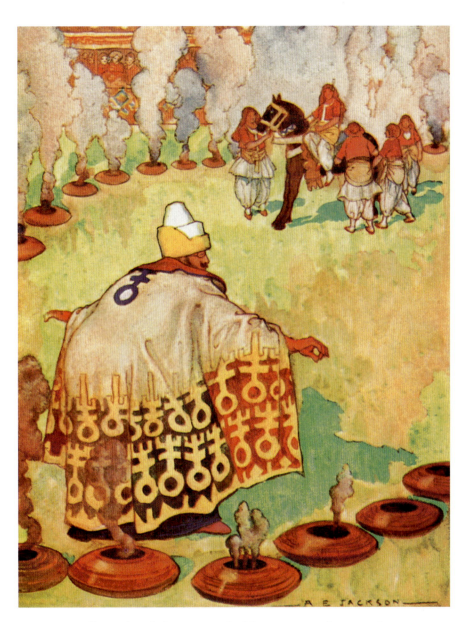

Soon both horse and riders were obscured
by dense smoke (page 226)

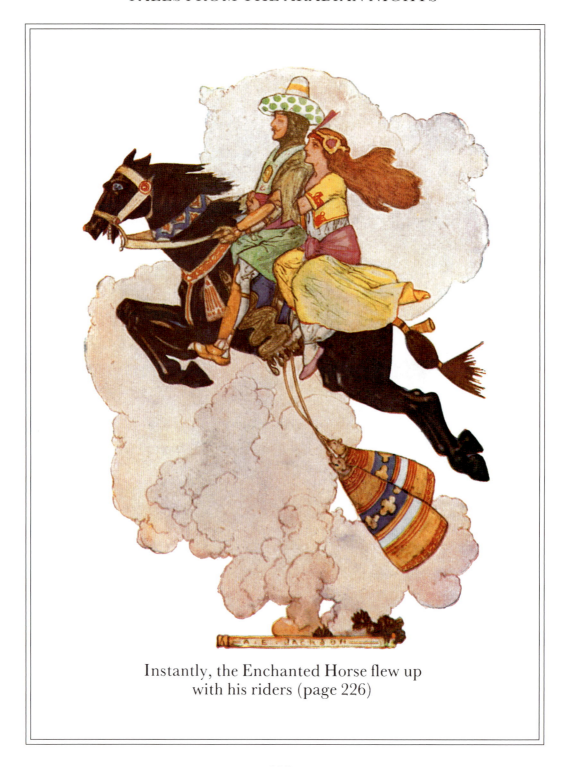

Instantly, the Enchanted Horse flew up
with his riders (page 226)

His beard had grown to quite a respectable length during his travels, and gave him a look of age and wisdom. Thus, he had only to exchange the robe of a dervish for that of a physician to be received at the palace of the Sultan with civility and respect.

"I have come to cure the Princess." he declared. "Many have tried and failed. If I do not succeed, you may cut off my head."

Some time had elapsed since a new physician had appeared at the palace, and the Sultan had begun to give up hope of the Princess's recovery. He therefore at once gave orders that this new physician, who showed so much faith in his healing powers, should be admitted to his presence. He then informed him that as the Princess of Bengal could not endure the sight of a physician, he would have to be content with a view of his patient through a lattice in an adjoining chamber to that which she occupied.

In this way, Prince Feroze-shah again caught sight of his beloved Princess after their long separation. She was sitting in a despondent attitude, and singing, with tears in her eyes, a mournful melody in which she lamented her sad fate in being separated from all she loved. It brought tears to his own eyes, and he determined to restore her to health and happiness at any cost.

With this intention, he told the Sultan that he now quite understood the nature of the complaint from which the Princess was suffering, and that he would undertake to cure her. But, he added, it was absolutely necessary to speak to her in private, and, if allowed to do so, he was convinced that he could overcome the violent dislike which she showed to any physician who approached her.

The Sultan was much cheered by this, and ordered that the new physician should be ushered into the presence of the Princess without delay.

As soon as the Princess caught sight of what she took to be yet another tiresome physician come to prescribe for her affected madness, she began to go through her usual performance of threatening to attack with teeth and fingernails anyone who attempted to come near enough to feel her pulse, or examine her eyes and complexion.

But the Prince, disregarding this, went straight to her, and, bending in salutation, said, in a low tone, for fear of listeners:

"Oh, my Princess, let your beautiful eyes pierce my disguise and see, in this pretend physician, the Prince of Persia, your faithful Feroze-shah, who has sought you in sorrow which is now turned into joy."

At the sound of the well-known voice, the Princess

almost fainted with rapture and relief. But, as the Prince warned her that it was possible that they might be under observation, she made an effort to appear calm. At the same time the Prince of Persia, while briefly acquainting her with his own doings and adventures, and listening to the Princess's story, took care to feel her pulse, and behave in every way like the physician he was impersonating.

He asked her if she knew what had become of the Enchanted Horse, by which he hoped they might both make their escape, but she could not tell him anything about it. Then, when a plan had been arranged between them, the Prince, thinking it unwise to pay too long a visit, left his supposed patient and went to make his report to the Sultan.

The latter was delighted to hear that a change for the better had already taken place, and promised the supposed physician a great reward if he succeeded in entirely restoring the Princess to health. On the next day, the Sultan paid her a visit, and when the lady, instead of biting the cushions and threatening to tear his beard out by the roots, received him in a most gracious and charming manner, he came away with the conviction that the disguised Prince was the greatest physician in the world. He even wished to have the preparations for the marriage resumed where they had been broken off, but the Prince declared that the Princess was not yet as perfectly recovered as he would wish. He asked the Sultan from what country she had come, and by what means she had journeyed to Kashmir, and the Sultan at once obliged him by relating the entire story of the Hindu and the Enchanted Horse, as far as he knew it.

Though he was unacquainted with the use and management of the horse, the Sultan had ordered it to be kept in his treasury as an object of curiosity and value.

At this, the pretended physician stroked his beard and assumed an expression of profound wisdom.

"Sire," he said, "I am inclined to think that the principal cause of the trouble is this very horse itself. The Princess, having ridden upon the horse, which, as your majesty knows, is enchanted, has herself been affected by the enchantment. In order, then, that the improvement which I have been so fortunate as to effect in her condition may continue and be made lasting, it is necessary that I should use a certain incense, the burning of which will disenchant the horse and so perfect the cure of the Princess. If your majesty wishes to see a wonderful sight, and give a great surprise and sensational entertainment to the people of the city, you will cause the Enchanted Horse to be brought to the great square before the Palace tomorrow, and leave the rest to me."

The Sultan signified his willingness to carry out the directions of this newest and greatest of physicians to the letter, and asked if the Princess should be present on the occasion.

"Most certainly," was the reply. "Let the lady be arrayed as a bride and adorned with jewels so as to set off her beauty to the greatest advantage."

Thus, early next day, the Enchanted Horse was, by order of the Sultan, brought with great ceremony and beating of drums to the square in front of the palace.

The news that something rare in the way of entertainment was to be provided had spread through the city, and so great a crowd assembled in the square that the Sultan's guards had all they could do to keep a space clear round the horse.

A gallery had been erected especially to accommodate the Sultan and his court, and, at the proper moment, the Princess of Bengal, accompanied by a band of ladies of high rank who had been especially chosen for this service, approached the horse, and was assisted to mount. The pretend physician then had a number of braziers of lighted charcoal placed at regular intervals round the horse, and into these he began solemnly to cast handfuls of incense. With downcast eyes, he paced three times round the horse within the circle made by the braziers, which now began to give off thick clouds of perfumed smoke.

In a few seconds these clouds became so thick that neither horse nor rider was visible. At this moment, for which he had been waiting, the Prince jumped nimbly up behind the Princess and, stretching out his hand, turned the right-hand peg. Instantly, the horse rose into the air, and, as the spectators gaped after it, the following words floated down and reached the ear of the Sultan.

"The next time the Sultan of Kashmir thinks of marrying a Princess who asks for protection, let him make sure that he has the lady's consent."

In this way the Princess of Bengal was rescued and brought the same day to Shiraz, the capital of Persia, where the return of the missing Prince with the lost Princess was greeted with joy.

The King of Persia at once sent an ambassador to the father of the Princess, to demand his consent to her marriage with Prince Feroze-shah. On that being given, the marriage was celebrated with much magnificence, and the Prince and Princess of Persia lived in wealth and happiness for many years after.

THE TALKATIVE
BARBER

n the city of Kashgar lived a tailor, who was of an extremely jovial and sociable disposition, and at whose shop a number of people were in the habit of meeting daily to exchange news and relate stories and adventures. Among them was a barber who had recently come to the city, but who had already made a reputation as a great talker. In fact, when he was present, there was little chance for any other tongue to wag.

One day, when the tailor was busily plying his needle as usual and listening to the talk going on around him, he observed a young man, handsome and well dressed, who appeared to be a stranger, and who walked with a limp.

The day was hot and the young man, pausing at the doorway of the shop, seemed glad to avail himself of the slight shelter which it afforded from the sun.

Seeing this, the tailor politely invited him to enter and rest for a while.

The young man thanked him, entered the shop,

and was about to accept the seat offered, when he caught sight of the barber, whose tongue, strange to say, was, for the moment, still.

At once, the pleasing expression of the stranger changed to one of horror and detestation, and, pointing to the barber, he said:

"There is the man to whom I owe my lameness, as well as the ruin of my peace and happiness. It was to escape from his detested presence that some time ago I left the city of Baghdad, and, after visiting several cities, arrived today at Kashgar. I hoped never to see him again, yet it appears that he has arrived here before me. I shall, therefore, at once quit this city, and seek some place where the sight of him will not revive unpleasant memories."

He turned to go, but the tailor and all those present, except the barber, who remained silent, with his eyes fixed on the ground, entreated the young man first to relate the reason for his animosity toward this individual.

"Willingly," he replied. Then, turning his back to the barber, he told the following story:

My father was a well-known and highly respected citizen of Baghdad. I was his only child, and on his death I inherited the whole of his large fortune. But, far from squandering it, I conducted myself so well as to gain the esteem of all who knew me.

Up to this time I had rather avoided feminine society, and had made up my mind to remain unmarried, as I considered a single life preferable.

One day, when I was walking in the street, I saw a number of ladies coming toward me, and, in order to avoid them, I turned into a narrow side street and sat down upon a bench. Opposite me in a window stood a number of very fine flowers. As I was admiring them, the window opened and a young lady appeared, whose beauty had a sudden and most extraordinary effect on me. She had a watering pot in her hand, and, as she watered the flowers, she glanced across at me and smiled. After she had tended her flowers, she shut the window and left me in a state of perturbation which I cannot describe.

A noise in the street brought me to my senses. I turned and saw one of the first Cadis of the city approaching, mounted on a mule, and accompanied by five or six of his people. He alighted at the door of the house where the young lady had opened the window, and from this I concluded he was her father.

I returned home in such a state of agitation, caused by this attack of love at first sight, that I was unable to eat or sleep. I became worse and worse until my relatives were alarmed. They sent for a certain wise woman, who was frequently consulted in domestic difficulties. She came and looked at me with a great deal of attention, afterwards begging to be left alone with me.

When the room was cleared, she seated herself near my pillow. "My son," said she, "you have hitherto persisted in concealing the cause of your illness, nor do I require you to confess it now. I have sufficient experience to discern that you are love-sick. I can probably accomplish your cure, provided you will tell me the name of the lady who has been able to make a conquest of one generally supposed to be a woman-hater."

I therefore described to her the street where I had seen the lady, and related all the circumstances of my adventure. "If you succeed," continued I, "in obtaining an interview for me with this enchanting beauty, you may rely on my continued gratitude and generosity."

"My son," replied the old woman, "I know the lady. You were quite right in supposing her to be the daughter of the principal Cadi in this city, and I am not surprised that you should have fallen in love with such a beautiful creature. At the same time, I must tell you that she is very proud and haughty. It is a pity you did not fall in love with someone else. Still, do not be downhearted. I will do my best to help."

So she left me in a condition between hope and fear, which resulted in another sleepless night.

When she returned the next day, it was with a very long face.

"My son," she said, shaking her head, "it was as I feared. I managed to gain an audience with the young lady and told her of the impression she had made upon you. But, as soon as I ventured to mention your desire for an interview, she showed annoyance and indignation.

" 'You are a very insolent old woman,' she said, 'and I will have nothing more to do with you if you say another word on the subject.' But, never mind," continued the old woman, "I am not at the end of my resources."

To cut a long story short, I will only say that the wise woman made several fruitless attempts to soften the heart of the haughty fair one, and I was reduced almost to skin and bone when one day the good soul came to give me new life.

"What present will you make me for the good news I bring you?" she whispered. I raised myself in my bed, and replied with feeling : "The gift shall be worthy of the occasion. What have you to tell me?"

"Yesterday," she resumed, "I went to the lady with whom you are in love, and found her in a good mood. I at first put on a mournful countenance, uttered a number of sighs, and shed some tears. 'My good mother,' said the lady, 'why are you in such affliction?' 'Alas! my dear lady,' replied I, 'I have just come from the young gentleman about whom I spoke to you the other day, and who is dying for love of you. Why are you so cruel to him?'

" 'I do not know,' said she, 'why you should accuse me of cruelty. How can I be blamed for his present condition?'

" 'What!' replied I, 'did I not tell you that he saw you watering your flowers and fell in love with the charms which your mirror reflects every day, And, what with thinking of you night and day, and being unable to eat or sleep, he is reduced to skin and bone. Indeed, unless some improvement takes place, I do not think he will live much longer.'

"This startled her, and I saw her turn very pale.

" 'Is what you say true?' she asked, 'and does his illness really proceed only from his love for me?'

" 'Ah, lady,' replied I, 'it is but too true!' 'And do you really think,' resumed she, 'that the hope of seeing and speaking to me would help his recovery?'

" 'Very probably,' said I. 'Then,' she replied, 'I

will allow him an interview; but he must not expect to marry me, unless my father gives his consent.'

" 'O, lady, 'said I, 'you are very good. I will go and tell the young gentleman that he is to have the delight of seeing and conversing with you.'

" 'I do not know,' said she, 'that I can fix a more convenient time for our interview than Friday next, during the midday prayer. Let him observe when my father goes to the mosque, and then let him come immediately to this house. We will converse together during the hour of prayer, and he must leave before my father returns.' "

While the good woman was talking, I began to feel better, and by the time she had concluded, I found myself quite recovered. "Take this," said I, giving her my purse full of gold. "To you alone I owe my cure."

On the appointed morning I rose early and spent some time reviewing my wardrobe and selecting the handsomest garments it contained. Then I decided that I need a shave, and ordered one of my slaves to seek a barber who was expert and quick.

The slave brought me this monstrous barber who is here present. After saluting me, he said: "My master, to judge by your looks I should say you are unwell." I replied that I was recovering from a very severe illness. "May Allah preserve you from all kinds of evils," continued he. "And now tell me what is your pleasure? I have brought my razors and my lancets. Do you wish me to shave or to bleed you?"

"Did I not tell you," returned I, "that I am recovering from an illness? I did not send for you to bleed me. Be quick and shave me, for I have an appointment precisely at noon."

The barber was very slow in spreading out his apparatus and preparing his razors. Instead of putting water into his basin, he drew out of his case a very neat astrolabe, which is an instrument for measuring the height of the sun, and, leaving the room, went into the court to take an observation.

On returning, he said "You will, no doubt, be glad to learn, sir, that this is the eighteenth day of the moon of Safar, and that the conjunction of Mars and Mercury signifies that you cannot choose a better time to be shaved than the present day and the present hour. But, on the other side, this conjunction carries with it a bad omen. It demonstrates to me that you will this day encounter a danger; not, indeed, a risk of losing your life, but the peril of an inconvenience which will remain with you all your days. You ought to thank me for warning you, and should be careful accordingly."

I was sincerely vexed at having fallen into the hands of this chatterbox of a barber. "I care very little," said I angrily, "for your advice or your predictions. You came here to shave me. Therefore, either perform your office or be gone, that I may send for another barber."

"My master," replied he, in an unconcerned tone which irritated me greatly, "what reason have you to be angry? Do you not know that all barbers are not like me, and that you would not find another like myself, even if you had him made expressly for you? You only asked for a barber, and in my person you see united the best barber of Baghdad, an experienced physician, a profound chemist, a never-failing astrologer, a finished grammarian, a perfect orator, a philosopher, a lawyer, a mathematician, who is also thoroughly accomplished in geometry, arithmetic, astronomy and algebra, an historian, a poet, and an architect. There is nothing in nature concealed from me; and I am prepared to take you under my protection and save you from all misfortunes with which the planets may threaten you."

Notwithstanding my anger, I could not help laughing at this speech. "When," I asked, "do you mean to stop chattering and begin to shave me?"

"Indeed," replied the barber, "you do me an

injury by calling me a chatterer, for you must know that everywhere I enjoy the honourable appellation of 'Silent'. I have six brothers, whom you might with some reason term chatterers. Their names are Bacbouc, Bakbara, Bakbac, Alcouz, Alnascher and Schacabac. One is hump-backed, one toothless, one half blind, one is quite blind, one is deaf, and the other has a defect in his speech. And they are all great talkers, but I, who am the youngest of the family, am very grave and sparing of my words."

"Give him three pieces of gold," I cried, losing all patience, "and send him away that I may be rid of him. I will not be shaved today."

"My master," cried the barber, at hearing this, "it was not I who came to seek you. It was you who ordered me to come, and, that being the case, I will not quit your house till I have shaved you."

He then began another speech, which lasted a full half-hour.

"In the name of Allah," I said to him, as he paused to take breath, "leave off the fine speeches, and despatch me quickly. I have an affair of the greatest importance which obliges me to go out at noon. Shave me at once or leave my house."

When he saw that I was really angry with him, he said: "O, master, do not be wrathful. I will begin

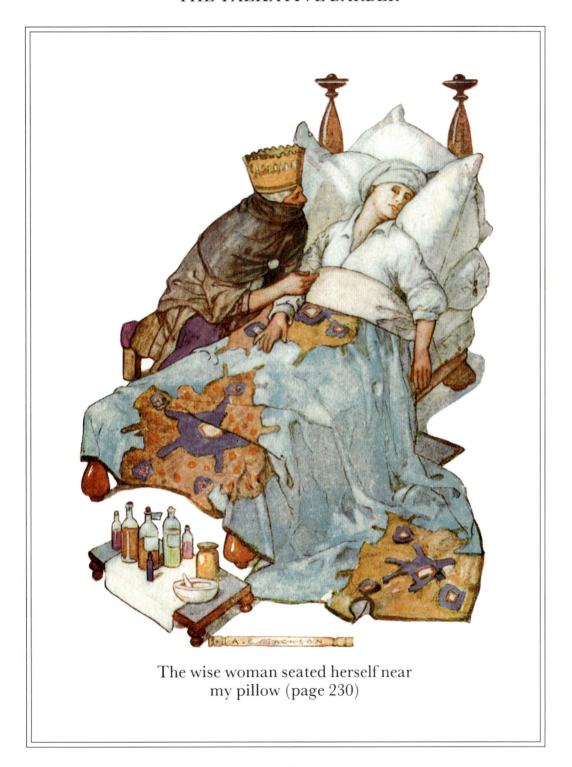

The wise woman seated herself near
my pillow (page 230)

"Be calm and you shall be shaved in a
moment," he said (page 235)

now." In fact, he washed my head and began to shave me, but he had not touched me four times with his razor when he stopped to say: "My master, you are hasty. You should abstain from these gusts of passion, which only do you harm."

"Go on shaving me," said I, "and speak no more. You ought to have finished long since."

"Moderate your impatience," replied he. "Perhaps you have not considered well what you are going to do. I wish you would tell me what this affair is about, which you are in such haste to tend to, and then I would give you my opinion on it. You have plenty of time, for it will not be noon for three hours."

"Finish shaving me at once," I exclaimed. But, instead of this, he seized his astrolabe a second time, and left me half shaved, to go and see precisely what hour it was.

"My master," said he on his return. "I was certain I was not mistaken. It wants three hours to noon, or all the rules of astronomy are false."

"Mercy of Allah!" cried I, "my patience is exhausted. I can hardly refrain from falling upon thee and strangling thee."

"Be calm, my master," said he coolly, "and you shall be shaved in a moment."

Saying this, he put the astrolabe in its case, took

his razor and began to shave me, but while he was shaving he could not help talking. "If," said he, "you would inform me what this affair is that will engage you at noon, I would give you some advice, which you might find serviceable."

To satisfy him, I told him that some friends expected me at noon, to give me a feast and rejoice with me on my recovery.

As soon as the barber heard me mention a feast, he exclaimed: "That reminds me that yesterday I invited four or five friends to come to my house today. But I had quite forgotten it, and have not made any preparations for them."

"Only be quick and finish shaving me," I replied, "and you shall have all the food that has been prepared for me today, and as much wine as you want."

He was not content to rely on my word. "May Allah recompense you," cried he. "But pray show me these provisions, that I may judge if there will be enough to regale my friends handsomely."

"I have," said I, "sufficient meat for four courses."

And I gave orders to a slave to produce the whole supply, together with four large jugs of wine.

"This is well," replied the barber, "but we shall want some fruit for dessert."

I told my slaves to give him what he wanted. He left off shaving me to examine each thing separately, and as this examination took up nearly half an hour, I stamped and raved with impatience, but the rascal did not hurry and fastes. At length, however, he again took up the razor and for a few minutes went on shaving me.

Then, stopping suddenly, he cried: "I should never have supposed that you had been of so liberal a turn. Certainly, I did not deserve the kindness you heap on me, and I assure you that I shall retain an eternal sense of my obligation, as I have nothing but what I get from generous people like yourself. In this I resemble Zantout, who rubs people at the bath, and Sali, who sells little burned peas in the streets, and Salouz, who sells beans, and Akerscha, who sells herbs, and Abou Mekares, who waters the streets to lay the dust, and Cassem, who belongs to the Caliph's guard. And yet they are all cheerful and contented, envying no one, and ready to dance and sing at every opportunity. If you will allow me, I will now show you exactly how Zantout sings and dances."

The barber sang the song and danced the dance of Zantout; and notwithstanding all I could say, he would not stop till he had given a similar imitation of

each of the men he had mentioned. After that he said:
"Sir I am going to invite all these good people to my
house, and, if you will take my advice, you will be of
our party and leave your friends, who are, perhaps,
great talkers, and will only disturb you by their
tiresome conversation."

Notwithstanding my anger, I could not avoid
laughing.

"I wish," said I, "that I had no other engagement.
Then I would gladly accept your proposal. As it is, I
must entreat you to excuse me. Finish shaving me
and hasten away, for, perhaps, your friends are
already waiting for you."

"Since you will not come with me," replied the
barber, "you must allow me to accompany you. I will
carry home the provisions you have given me; my
friends shall eat of them, if they like, and I will return
immediately."

"In the name of Allah!" I exclaimed, "go to your
friends, eat and drink, and enjoy yourselves, and
leave me at liberty to go to mine. The place where I
am going is not one in which you can be received."

"On the contrary, my master," he replied, "you
will much oblige your friends by taking with you a
man like me, who has the art of entertaining and
making people merry. Say what you will, I am

resolved to go, in spite of your request otherwise."

It was now almost the moment to set out. I determined, therefore, to appear as if I agreed to everything. So, when he had at last finished shaving me, I said: "Take some of my people with you to carry these provisions to your home and then return hither. I will not go without you."

He accordingly went out, and I finished dressing as quickly as possible. I only waited till I heard the last summons to prayers, and then set forth on my errand. But this wretched barber, who seemed aware of my intention, took care only to accompany my people to within sight of his own house. As soon as he had seen them go in, he concealed himself at the corner of the street to observe and follow me. Accordingly, when I got to the door of the Cadi, I turned round and was enraged to catch sight of him at the end of the street.

The Cadi's door was half open, and when I went in I found the old woman waiting to conduct me into the presence of the object of my admiration. But I had hardly commenced a conversation with her, when we heard a great noise in the street. The young lady ran to the window, and, looking through the blinds, perceived that the Cadi, her father, was already returning from prayers. I also looked out, and saw the barber seated opposite the house.

I had now two subjects for alarm, the arrival of the Cadi and the presence of the barber. The young lady quieted my fears on the one subject by telling me that her father very rarely came up to her apartment. All the same, she had prepared the means of my escape in case of necessity, but the presence of that abominable barber at the end of the street, caused me great uneasiness.

As soon as the Cadi had returned home, he began beating a slave who had disobeyed him. The slave uttered loud cries, which could be plainly heard in the street. The barber thought I was the person who was being ill treated, and that these were my cries. Fully persuaded of this, he began to call out as loudly as he could. He tore his clothes, threw dust upon his head and shouted for help to people nearby, who came running out of their houses. They inquired what was the matter. "Matter enough," exclaimed the barber. "They are murdering my master."

He then ran to my house and returned, followed by all my servants armed with sticks. They knocked furiously at the door of the Cadi, who sent a slave to know what the noise meant. But the slave returned in a state of alarm to his master.

"My lord," said he, "a number of men are trying to

force their way into the house, and are already beginning to break open the door."

The Cadi himself ran to the door and inquired what the people wanted. His venerable appearance did not inspire my people with any respect, and they shouted insolently: "What has our master done to you that you are trying to murder him?"

"My good friends," replied the Cadi, "why should I murder your master, whom I do not even know? My door is open. You may come in and search my house."

"You have been beating him," said the barber. "I heard his cries not a minute ago."

"But how," persisted the Cadi, "can your master have offended me, that I should ill-treat him thus? Is he in my house? And if he is here, how could he get in, or who could have admitted him?"

"You will not make me believe you, for all your great beard, you old villain!" cried the barber. "Your daughter and our master are in love with each other and arranged to meet during the midday prayers. You must have found this out and returned quickly. You surprised him here and ordered your slaves to beat him unmercifully. Set him free at once, or we will come and take him."

"There is no occasion," said the Cadi, "to make

such a riot. If what you say is true, you have only to go in and search for your master."

As soon as the Cadi had spoken these words, the barber and my servants burst into the house and began to ransack every corner in search of me.

As I had heard every word the barber said to the Cadi, I tried to find some place in which I might conceal myself. The only hiding place I could discover was a large, empty chest, into which I crept and shut the lid down upon myself. After the barber had searched every other place, he at last came into the apartment where I lay. He ran at once to the chest and opened it, and finding me crouching there, he took it up and carried it away on his head. He rushed down the staircase into a court, and so reached the street.

As he was carrying me along, the lid of the chest unfortunately opened. I had not resolution enough to bear the shame and disgrace of my exposure to the crowd who followed us, and jumped out so hastily that I hurt myself seriously, and have been lame ever since.

I did not at first feel the full extent of the injury I had suffered, and was able to get up and run away from the people who were laughing at me. I scattered among them a handful or two of gold and silver, and, while they were stopping to pick it up, made my escape by hurrying through several quiet streets. But the wretched barber followed me closely and never once lost sight of me, and, as he followed me, he continued calling aloud: "Stop, my master! Why do you run so fast? All that has happened to you is your own fault, and I know not what would have become of you if I had not determined to follow you. I pray you, wait for me."

This put me into such a rage that I could have stopped and strangled him, but that would only have increased my difficulties. I therefore went into an inn, the master of which was known to me, and said, "In the name of Allah! Prevent that mad fellow from following me in here."

He promised to do so and he kept his word, though not without great difficulty. As it was, this abominable barber abused me violently for what he termed my ingratitude, and told everyone he met the great service he had performed for me.

Thus I got rid of him. I knew that if I returned to my house, either the barber would pester me to death, or else I should be driven to kill him. Therefore, in spite of the poorness of the accommodation, I remained at the inn until I had to some extent recovered from my injury. But, after what had happened to me, I determined to leave the city.

So, having arranged my affairs, I set out from Baghdad and arrived here. I had every reason to hope I would be free from this detestable barber in a country so distant from my own. You may judge of my feelings when I now discover, in your company, the man who is responsible both for my lameness and for the abrupt ending of a love affair which might have terminated in a happy marriage, and who has also made me an object of ridicule to the whole city."

With that, the young man went out.

"All the same," remarked the barber as soon as the other was out of hearing. "I maintain that I was perfectly right in acting as I did. And he who has just left us is the most ungrateful of men."

THE DREAM

nce, long ago, there lived in Baghdad a rich merchant who lost all his money by spending it foolishly. Eventually, he became so poor that he could only live by doing the hardest work for the smallest amount of money.

One night, tired and depressed, he fell into a deep sleep and, as he slept, he heard a voice saying to him, "Your fortune lies in Cairo. Go and seek it there."

The next morning, without delay, he set off for Cairo and, after journeying for many weeks and enduring much hardship on the way, he arrived there. Night had fallen and as he could not afford to stay at an inn, he lay down to sleep in the courtyard of a local mosque.

Now, it so happened that a band of robbers entered the mosque and from there broke into a nearby house. Awakened by the noise, the owners of the house shouted for help, whereupon the thieves ran off. Presently, the chief of police and his men arrived on the scene and made their way into the mosque. Upon finding the merchant from Baghdad in the courtyard, they seized him and beat him with their clubs until he was crying for mercy. Then they threw him into gaol.

Three days later, the chief of police ordered his men to bring the stranger before him.

"Where do you come from?" asked the chief.

"From Baghdad," said the merchant.

"And what has brought you to Cairo?"

"I heard a voice in my sleep telling me 'Your fortune lies in Cairo. Go and seek it there.' But when I came to Cairo, the fortune I was promised turned out to be the beating I received from your men."

When the chief of police heard this he burst out laughing.

"Know then, you fool," he cried, "that I, too, have heard a voice in my sleep, not just once but on three separate occasions. The voice said 'Go to Baghdad, and in a cobbled street lined with tall palm trees, you will find a three storey house, with a courtyard lined with green marble. At the far end of the garden there is a fountain of white marble; under this fountain a large sum of money is buried. Go there and dig it up.' But did I go? Of course not. Yet, fool that you are, you have come all this way on the strength of a silly dream."

Then the chief of police gave the merchant some money.

"Here," he said, "take this. Perhaps it will help you on the way back to your own country."

From the policeman's description, the merchant immediately realized that the house and garden were his own. He took the money and, with all speed, set out on his homeward journey.

As soon as he reached his house he went into the garden, dug beneath the fountain and, to his amazement, found a chest filled with silver and gold.

Thus the words of his dream were wondrously fulfilled, and Allah made the ruined merchant rich again.

THE DONKEY

ne day, two rogues were sitting by the side of the road when they saw a simple looking fellow leading a donkey on the end of a long rope.

"Watch this," said one to the other. "I will take that beast and, by so doing, will make a fool of its master. Come along and you will see what I mean."

He followed quietly along behind the simple fellow without making a sound, and unfastened the rope for the donkey and put it around his own neck. He then jogged along in the donkey's place, while his friend made off with the donkey.

Suddenly, the thief with the donkey's rope around his neck, stopped dead in his tracks and refused to go any further. The silly fellow, feeling the sudden pull on the rope, looked over his shoulder and was amazed to find that his donkey had changed into a man.

"Who is heaven's name are you?" he cried.

"Sir," the thief replied, "I am your donkey and the

story I have to tell you is quite extraordinary. It all happened one day when I came home miserably drunk – as I usually did. My poor old mother scolded me terribly and begged me to mend my ways. But I took my stick and beat her. In her anger she called down Allah's curse upon me, and I was at once changed into the donkey that has served you faithfully all these years. My mother must have taken pity on me, though, and prayed to the Almighty to change me back into a human shape."

"Good heavens!" cried the simple fellow, who believed every word of the rascal's story. "Please forgive all that I have done to you and all the hardships you put up with in my service."

He let the robber go and returned home, bewildered and very upset.

"What has come over you and where is your donkey?" asked his wife when she saw him.

He told her the incredible story.

"Allah will be angry with us," the woman cried, wringing her hands, "for having used a human being so cruelly." And she fell down on her knees and prayed for forgiveness.

For several days afterwards, the simple fellow stayed around at home. At last his wife told him to go out and buy another donkey so that he could start to do some work again. He went off to the market, and as he was taking a look at the array of animals that were for sale, he was astonished to see his own donkey among them. When he had made absolutely sure that the beast was, without doubt, his own, he whispered in its ear, "Well, you old scoundrel. Have you been drinking and beating your mother again? Upon my life, I will not buy you *this* time!"

He returned, followed by my servants all
armed with sticks (page 244)

"I jumped out hastily and hurt
my leg" (page 246)